Thomas Maurice

Poems and Miscellaneous Pieces

with a free translation of the Oedipus tyrannus of Sophocles

Thomas Maurice

Poems and Miscellaneous Pieces
with a free translation of the Oedipus tyrannus of Sophocles

ISBN/EAN: 9783337285074

Printed in Europe, USA, Canada, Australia, Japan

Cover: Foto ©Andreas Hilbeck / pixelio.de

More available books at **www.hansebooks.com**

P O E M S

A N D

MISCELLANEOUS PIECES,

W I T H A

FREE TRANSLATION

O F T H E

OEDIPUS TYRANNUS OF SOPHOCLES.

B Y

THE REV. THOMAS MAURICE, A. B.

O F

UNIVERSITY COLLEGE, OXFORD.

L O N D O N,

Printed for the A U T H O R;

And sold by J. Dodsley, Pall-mall; G. Kearsly, in Fleet-street;
Messrs. Fletcher, Prince, Parker and Bliss, Oxford; and
Messrs. Woodyer and Merryl, in Cambridge.

M.DCC.LXXIX.

TO HIS GRACE

THE DUKE OF MARLBOROUGH.

My Lord,

To animate mankind to the practice of virtue, and the conqueſt of thoſe paſſions which are moſt detrimental to ſociety, by holding forth examples taken from real life, either of vice degraded or triumphant virtue, hath ever been the chief aim of thoſe who duly conſidered the nature and origin of theatrical compoſition. While Comedy holds the mirror to folly, it is the office of Tragedy to expoſe to public deteſtation thoſe vices, to which the diſtinguiſhed rank of the offender, or the nature of the offence itſelf, ſanctified by the "ſtupet in titulis" of popular deluſion, may have given a long and ſecure dominion over the human mind.

Sophocles, my Lord, hath given us in the following pages a lively and pathetic inſtance of the deſtructive nature of ambition, of the inſtability of human grandeur, and of the diſaſters too generally conſequent when the paſſions are not under the due ſubordination of reaſon. I am convinced I ſhall offend no perſon except yourſelf, when I add that the ſteady and tranquil happineſs which hath ever attended your Grace in the exerciſe of every ſocial and domeſtic virtue, and the univerſal reſpect paid to that integrity which neither intereſt could ever allure, nor ambition ever ſhake from the baſis whereon it is fixed, will be the beſt proof and the ſtrongeſt confirmation of the doctrine which this great maſter of tragic writing and morality hath thus endeavoured to eſtabliſh.

At a period when the moſt ſolemn ties, both religious and civil, are treated with ſuch avowed contempt, to behold thoſe, who are moſt eminent among our nobility, ſteadily adhering to the dictates of virtue, and ſetting ſo conſpicuous an example of parental duty and conjugal affection, muſt, while it abaſhes the front of vice, excite in the breaſt of every good man the ſublimeſt ſatisfaction, accompanied with the heartieſt wiſhes for its long continuance among mankind.

I have the honour to be,

My Lord,

Your Grace's moſt obliged

And moſt devoted ſervant,

Woodford, 15th June, 1779.

THOMAS MAURICE.

P R E-

P R E F A C E.

MOST of the following Poems have been already submitted to the inspection of the public: under the sanction, however, of so many respectable names, and with the alterations recommended to the Author by many judicious friends, they will perhaps have a better plea to their attention.

To urge, that, of the miscellaneous pieces in this collection, the greater part are juvenile compositions, and that the translation itself is but a continuation of those endeavours which were exerted at a time of life when his ambition indeed was awakened, but his judgment immature, would be an excuse very inadequate to their defects. He is inclined rather to submit them with those defects to the consideration of the reader, and await the sentence, if not of candour, at least of impartiality.

With respect to the EPISTOLARY VERSES, the Author has only to intreat the forgiveness of those to whom they have at different times been sent for the liberty his ambition led him to take of uniting their names with his own in a work which, otherwise perhaps, might share the fate common to the poetical productions of the age.

The Poem of HERO AND LEANDER is not a regular translation of any part of Moschus; neither is the Eastern Elegy, entitled HINDA, offered to the public as a particular imitation of any Asiatic poet: the first was composed as an exercise at school, and the latter was written when the imagination of the Author had been animated with the perusal of those beautiful specimens of Eastern poetry, lately given to the world by Mr. Jones, and Mr. Richardson.

THE PROSPECT OF LIFE was in its original form a paraphrase of a Grecian Chorus: the plan has been since enlarged, but the picture perhaps is too gloomy not to meet with censure.

A writer, who is ambitious of general applause, should never engage in disputes of party: but the present unhappy contest in America is certainly a subject for too extensive concern to fix the stigma

of

of faction on the bard who laments it. The VERSES therefore written at that æra when thofe fatal hoftilities commenced, will require lefs apology, becaufe they exprefs, though in an unworthy manner, the fentiments of every true lover of his country.

The Tragedy of the TRACHINIANS of Sophocles was performed in the original Greek by the fcholars of a gentleman, to whom the Author with gratitude acknowledges himfelf indebted for his own education. The lines here publifhed, were meant to have been recited, previous to the performance. Though, for fome reafons, they were not fpoken, he was unwilling to refufe the requeft of thofe, who, from being concerned in that performance, had a right to demand the perufal of them. If they meet with their approbation, he fhall not be anxious whether or not they can ftand the teft of feverer criticifm.

The Poems that follow have been already honoured with a public perufal, and with fome fhare of the public applaufe.

To the Tranflation itfelf are prefixed a few prefatory pages, which will explain the plan on which the Tranflator has proceeded. That fome of the fpeeches toward the end of the Tragedy appear immoderately long, though fome cenfure may be due to his own want of ability to find words fufficiently expreffive of the original idea, is partly to be afcribed to the cuftom of the Greek dramatic writers, who made the αγγελος relate the moft interefting events of the play, and often difplayed in their fpeeches, as well as in thofe of the principal characters, which are likewife generally extended to a confiderable length, all that vigour of genius that fo ftrongly marks the tragical writers of antiquity.

Some apology is neceffary for the delay in the publication of this book: but thofe who are acquainted with the difficulties and delays that attend works of this kind when the Author cannot be on the fpot, will form in their own minds a better excufe for him, than any he himfelf can offer.

S U B-

SUBSCRIBERS NAMES.

A

RIGHT Hon. Earl of Abingdon

Pell Akehurst, Efq. Fellow of King's College, Cambridge

Rev. Charles Allcock, M. A. Fellow of New College, Oxford

Rev. M. Alexander, B. A. Univerfity College, Oxford, two copies

Jofeph Amphlett, Efq. Dudley, Worcefterfhire

Mr. Angell

Richard Archdale, Efq. Inner Temple, London

Adam Afkew, Efq. Fellow Commoner of Emanuel College, Cambridge, two copies

B

Right Rev. the Lord Bifhop of Bangor

Moft noble the Marquis of Blandford, two copies

John Badely, M. D. Chelmsford, Effex

Mrs. Mary Barnadifton

David Batfon, Efq. Hatton-ftreet

Robert Beachcroft, Efq.

John Blackburn, Efq.

Henry Bolton, Efq. Middle Temple

Hugh Bateman, Efq. Lincoln's-inn, two copies

Richard Bateman, Efq. gentleman commoner of Univerfity College, Oxford, two copies

John Bayley, M. D. of Chichefter, Suffex

Thomas Charles Beaumont, Efq. Univerfity College, Oxford, two copies

Edward Buckley Batfon, Efq.

Rev. Miles Beever, B. A. Univerfity-College, Oxford, two copies

Jonathan Bell, Efq. Hertford

Theophilus Biddolph, Efq. gentleman commoner of Univerfity College, Oxford

Elifha Bifcoe, Efq.

Richard Birch, Efq. fellow commoner of Corpus Chrifti College, Cambridge

Rev. William Bennet, M. A. Fellow of Emanuel College, Cambridge

Rev. Mr. Booth, B. D. Fellow of Merton College, Oxford

Thomas Borrow, Efq. of Caftlefields, Derbyfhire, two copies

Thomas Borrow, Efq. of Univerfity College, Oxford, two copies

Daniel Braithwaite, Efq. General Poft-office, London

Mr. J. Braithwaite

Robert Bree, B. A. Univerfity College, Oxford

Jonas Langford Brooke, Efq. gentleman commoner of Magdalen College, Oxford, two copies

Rev. Mr. Brundifh, M. A. Fellow of Caius College, Cambridge, two copies

Edward Perry Buckley, Efq. gentleman commoner of Chrift Church College, Oxford, two copies

Francis Bullock, Efq. Ardington, Berks

Richard Byron, Efq. Hertford

Rev. John Buckner, A. M. Prebendary of Chichefter

C

Hon. Edward Seymour Conway

Rev. James Camplin, B. A. Fellow of St. John's College, Oxford

John C. rew, Esq. gentleman commoner of Oriel College, Oxford

N'r John Carr, Hertford

Rev. William Coates, M. A. Fellow of University College, Oxford

Rev. William Cokayne, D. D. Hertford

John Cook, Esq. gentleman commoner of Brazen Nose College, Oxford, two copies

Mr. Collins

Richard Cooke, Esq. Cheshunt

William Cooke, Esq. Woodford

Miss Hannah Cooke, Woodford

Rev. John Coulson, M. A. Senior Fellow of University College, Oxford

Rev. Mr. Clarke, M. A. Fellow of University College, Oxford

James Crawford, Esq Dublin

Rev. Mr. Crofts, M. A. Fellow of University College, Oxford

—— Crawley, Esq. University College, Oxford, two copies

Alexander Croke, Esq. gentleman commoner of Oriel College, Oxford

Richard Cutler, Esq. Hertford

James Cutler, Esq. Fellow of St. John's College, Oxford

William Cunningham, Esq. gentleman commoner of Christ Church College, Oxford, two copies

Chaloner Chute, Esq. fellow commoner of Clare Hall, Cambridge

Peter Cazalet, Esq. Woodford

D

Samuel Dennis, D. D. President of St. John's College, Oxford

Stephen Demainbray, L. L. D. Richmond, Surry

Rev. Thomas Davison, A. B. Rector of Crow-math, Berkshire

Mrs Davison, Reading, Berkshire

William Dacre, Esq. Kirklinton, Cumberland

William Dean, Esq. Dublin

Stephen D. mainbray, Esq. Fellow of Exeter College, Oxford

Jonathan Dickinson, Esq.

Mr. F. Dickinson

N. Dalton, Esq. Clare hall, Cambridge

William Dodd, Esq. Oriel College, Oxford

Charles Du-beilamy, Esq.

Mr Charles Dicker

Thomas Davies, Esq.

Henry Dunster, Esq. Hertford

E

Charles Echlin, Esq. Dublin

Lieutenant Edwards

John Michael Evans, Esq. Harford-street, May-fair

Mrs. Evans, ditto

Rev. Joseph Eyre, B. A. Rector of Purlock, Northamptonshire

F

Hon. Thomas Fitz Maurice

James Farrer, Esq.

John Farhill, A. B. Fellow of Bennet College, Cambridge

Rev. William Finch, L. L. D. St. John's College, Oxford

William Finch, Esq. of Shelford-hall, Cambridgeshire, four copies

Rev. Philip Fisher, A. M. Fellow of University College, Oxon, two Copies

—— Fleming, Esq.

Frederick Flood, Esq Dublin

John Foote, Esq. gentleman commoner of University College, Oxford

Robert Foote, Esq. University Coll. Oxford

William Fowlis, Esq. gentleman commoner of ditto, two copies

Francis Ford, Esq. fellow commoner of St. John's College, Cambridge

Rev. Mr. Ford, B. D. Baliol College, Oxford

Thomas Charles Fountayne, Esq. fellow commoner of Clare-hall, Cambridge, 2 copies

Rev. Nat. Forster, D. D. Rector of St. James's, Colchester

G

John Goddard, Esq. of Woodford-hall, Essex

Colonel Goate,

Anthony Grayson, Esq. four copies

Rev. Robert Graham, D. D. of Netherby, Cumberland

Mrs. Graham

Charles Graham, Esq. gentleman commoner of Magdalen College, Oxford, two copies

James Graham, ditto, two copies

Rev. Charles Graham, Hartingfordbury, Herts

Thomas Græme, Esq. gentleman commoner of Queen's College, Oxford

Thomas Greet, Esq. gentleman commoner of University College, Oxford, two copies

Thomas Grove, Esq. ditto, two copies

William Gregory, Esq. of Baliol Coll. Oxfd.

G. Gun, Esq. gentleman commoner of Magdalen College, Oxford

Leſlie Grove, Eſq.

H

Right Hon. Earl of Harcourt
Hon. and Rev. John Hewit
Hon. Joſeph Hewit
Rev. George Horne, D. D. Preſident of Magdalen College, and Vice Chancellor of the Univerſity of Oxford
—— Haggard, Eſq. Emanuel College, Cambridge
Mathew Hall, Eſq. Univerſity College, Oxford, two copies
Henry Harford, Eſq. gentleman commoner of Exeter College, Oxford, two copies
James Hammerſly, Eſq.
·Rev. Mr. Heap, Chicheſter
Thomas Hornſby, Eſq. Univerſity College, Oxford
William Humphries, Eſq. gentleman commoner of Univerſity College, Oxford
Francis Hutchinſon, M. D. Dublin

J

Right Hon. Earl of Inchiquin
William Jones, Eſq. F. R. S. Fellow of Univerſity College, Oxford
Clarke Jervoiſe, Eſq. Woodford
Mr. Jacques, Chicheſter
Samuel Johnſon, L. L. D.
William Julius, Eſq. Hampſtead
John Jones, Eſq. Inner Temple
—— Jurdan, Eſq.

K

Right Hon. Lord Killmorey, two copies
Richard Gervas Karr, Eſq.
Thomas Norbury Kerby, Eſq. gentleman commoner of Trinity College, Oxford
Samuel Killderbee, Eſq. Univerſity College, Oxford
Rev. J. Kilpin, Woodford
Edward Keepe, Eſq. ditto

L

Right Hon. Lord Lyfford, Lord Chancellor of Ireland
Right Hon. Lord Lyttelton
Hon. William Legge, All Soul's College, Oxford
Hon. Heniage Legge, Student of Chriſt Church
Right Hon. Lord George Lennox
James Haughton Langtton, Eſq. Woodford
William Lewis, Eſq. gentleman commoner of Univerſity College, Oxford, two copies

Mr. Lewis, Hertford
John Ludford, Eſq.
Richard Warburton Lytten, Eſq. Bath
Mr. Lyon, Bath
Rev. John Lyſter, A. M. Univerſity College, Oxford
William Lyſter, Eſq. Dublin
William D. Lyſter, Eſq ditto
Henry Lyſter, Eſq ditto
Rev. J. S Lovat, A. M. Rector of Loughton, Eſſex, two copies

M

His Grace the Duke of Marlborough, two copies
Her Grace the Dutcheſs of Marlborough, two copies
Hon. Jacob Marſham
William Maſon, Eſq. Emanuel College, Cambridge
Martin Madan. Eſq. Middle Temple
John Maddion, Eſq.
George Maddiſon, Eſq.
John Edward Maddocks, Eſq. gentleman commoner of Magdalen College, Oxford
Chriſtopher Thompſon Maling, Eſq.
Thomas Meade. Eſq. Woodford
John Milles, Eſq. F. R. S.
Mr. W. Maurice, Hertford
William Julius Mickle
John Monro, M. D.
John Monro, A. B. Fellow of St. John's College, Oxford
Charles Monro, Eſq. Middle Temple
Thomas Monro, Eſq. Oriel College, Oxford
James Mowbray, Eſq. Woodford
Captain Henry Murray
John Monins, Eſq. Woodford
John Chardin Muſgrave, Eſq. two copies
Chriſtopher Muſgrave, Eſq. Oriel College, Oxford

N

His Grace the Duke of Northumberland, two copies
Hon. Robert Needham
Pendock Neale, Eſq. gentleman commoner of Magdalen College, Oxford, two copies
Mr. J. Neave
John Nicol, Eſq. Fellow of St. John's, Oxford
John Newman, Eſq. Fellow of New College, Oxford
Mr. Nicholſon, Chicheſter

O

Robert Orme, Eſq. Hertford
James Oliver, Eſq.

P

Right Hon. Earl Percy
Right Hon. Lord Algernon Percy
Sir Charles Palmer, Bart.
Rev. Samuel Parr, A. M. master of the grammar school, Norwich
Francis Parrot, Esq. Birmingham
Joseph Payne, Esq. L. L. B. Inner Temple
Rev. Henry Peach, B. D. Fellow of St. John's, Oxford
John Peachey, Esq. Middle Temp'e
Major Thomas Pearson
John Penn, Esq. Clare-hall, Cambridge
Rev. Thomas Percy, D. D. Dean of Carlisle
Rev. Mr. Perry, Dudley, Worcestershire
Captain Richard Pierce
Rev. Charles Plucknett, B. D. Fellow of St. John's College, Oxford
Edward Poore, Esq. F. R. S. Lincoln's-Inn
James Pope, A. B. Fellow of St. John's College, Oxford
Edward Pole, Esq. University College, two copies
Mr. Popplewell, Woodford
John Price, Esq; Nebworth, Herts
Christopher Puller, Esq. Woodford

R

Sir Joshua Reynolds
Thomas Rackett, A. B. Univ. Col. Oxford
Rev. John Ravenhill, B. A. ditto
G. J. Reddel, Esq. gentleman commoner of Magdalen College, Oxford
Richard Richardson, A. B. University College, Oxford
Henry Richardson, Esq. University College, Oxford, two copies
Mr. Richards
Rev. Mr. Robinson, Fellow of Clare Hall, Cambridge
Rev. D. Roderick, A. M.
Rev. Mr. Robinson, M. A. Merton College, Oxford
Rev. Moreton Rockliffe, A. M. Woodford

S

Right Rev. the Lord Bishop of St. Asaph
Right Hon. Earl of Surry, two copies
Hon. Henry St. John, two copies
Thomas Sanden, M. D. Chichester
John Smith, Esq. of Coomb-Hay, Somerset shire, two copies
William Scott, Esq. Fellow of University College, Oxford, and Camden's professor of history
John Scott, Esq. of Amwell, Hertfordshire
Robert Snow, Esq. Saville Row
Rev. Charles Smith, L. L. B. Chichester
Charles Geo. Starck, A. B. Mert. Col. Oxford
Rowland Stephenson, Esq. Queen's-square
Mrs. Stephenson

Edward Stephenson, Esq. gentleman commoner of Queen's College, Oxford, 2 copies
Robert Steel, Esq. Middle Temple
—— Sampson, Esq. Emanuel Col. Cambr.
Charles Stanhope, Esq. University College, Oxford
Thomas Steel, Esq. Chichester
Walter Stirling, Esq. Harpur-street
John Stuart, Esq. gentleman commoner of Oriel College, Oxford
Geo. Sumner, Esq. fellow commoner of Emanuel College, Cambridge
Humphrey Sumner, A. M. Fellow of King's College, Cambridge
Captain R. B. Supple
John Surtees, A. B. University Col. Oxford
Rev. J. Shepard, M. A. Rector of Woodford, Essex, two copies
—— Stannsford, Esq. Woodford, Essex
Rev. William Shillito, Colchester
Master R. Skinner, Eton School
James Street, Esq. Woodford

T

Right Hon. Lord Viscount Turnour, Trinity College, Oxford
Robert Tundall, Esq. fellow commoner of Trinity College, Cambridge
Thomas Todd, Esq.
Nathaniel Thomas, Esq. Woodford
Johnson Towers, E s. Tunbridge

Sir James Wright,
Rev. Nathan. verell, D. D. Dean of Hereford, and Master of University College, Oxford, two copies
Rev. Benjamin Wheeler, D. D. Canon of Christ Church College, Oxford, and Regius Professor of Divinity
Mr. Wainwright
Rev. William Walker, M. A. Rector of Wyke, near Chichester
Rev. John Waters, L. L. B. St. John's College, Oxford
Mr. Wallace, Fellow of Bennet College, Oxford
Rev. Richard Webster, A. B. Fellow of St. John's, Oxford
Charles Webber, Esq. Student of Christ Church College, Oxford
—— Welles, Esq. Oriel College, Oxford
Mr. R. Welles
Thomas Willes, Esq. L. L. B. University College, Oxford
John Wilkinson, M. D. F. R. S. Woodford
Francis Woodhouse, Esq.
John Woodhouse, Esq.
Edmund Woods, Esq. Lincoln's-inn

3

C O N T E N T S.

To SAMUEL JOHNSON, L.L.D.

WHILE Britain's lofty bards his thoughts engage,
Will Johnfon fmile on this ignobler page?
From thee her flame my infant fancy caught,
And kindled at thy page the glowing thought;
Learn'd, by thy light, her fteady courfe to guide,
Tempt the rough fhore, and brave the deepening tide.

   What equal tribute fhall the mufe prepare;
What heights of rapid fong unufual dare?
But when her hand hath fwept the nobleft wires,
Above her boldeft flights thy praife afpires:
The wife, the virtuous venerate thy name;
This is thy praife, and this the nobleft fame.

   Oh truly great! whofe generous, active mind
Scorns ev'ry labour but to blefs mankind!
Thine the high tafk a nation to reform,
The rifing race with virtuous hopes to warm;

B

With

With folly's fons eternal war to wage,
And lafh the crimes of an abandon'd age.

Befet with ills, opprefs'd by namelefs woes,
Superior to their rage, thy genius rofe :
Unable thefe to crufh thy great defign,
To damp thy piety, thy thoughts confine!
On wealth, and power, thy fteadfaft foul looks down,
Regardlefs if the mighty fmile or frown.
Guilt is thy foe, guilt open, or conceal'd,
And none are fafe whom virtue does not fhield :
When in her caufe thou draw'ft the righteous fword,
It wounds, alike, the peafant and the lord.

By thee refin'd, to full perfection brought,
We rival Greece in language, as in thought ;
Genius foars bolder, fancy brighter fhines,
And manlier vigour animates our lines.
Let blockheads rail, whofe precepts, wifely, teach
To call *obfcure*, what dullnefs cannot reach :
Thy labour'd volume claims our nobleft praife,
That loftier fenfe in loftier found conveys.
How fweet, how ftrong, the polifh'd periods roll,
With thoughts that rouze, tranfport, convince the foul!

A

But.

But are there some, the steady foes of worth,
Still prompt to give the embryo falshood birth,
Who strive to blacken thy illustrious name,
By each mean art that dark revenge can frame;
Attack the firmnes of an honest heart,
That scorns, alike, the knave's or villain's part;
Faction's base sons, who principle disdain,
Or know no principle, but that of gain?
If such there are, ev'n these thou can'st despise,
Ev'n these thy fix'd integrity defies:
Thy fame shall flourish when their mem'ries rot,
Their rage, their writings, like their names, forgot.

What bold, ambitious hopes, my bosom warm,
Oft' as my eyes behold thy honour'd form;
As all the labours of thy life I trace,
Thy glory, and the glory of our race!
Thy mind, retaining still her wonted fires,
With added years increasing strength acquires:
Vig'rous, as when to Juvenal's manly page
Thy muse congenial gave rekindled rage.
But thy ambition boasts a nobler aim,
Than man's applauses, and the bubble, fame;

Anxious

Anxious to gain, and eager to fecure,

That brighter meed to patient virtue fure;

Thine are the joys, that animate the juft,

And lift the foul above its kindred duft :　.

Ev'n here, the dazzling fcenes entrance thy fight,

While confcience gives a feraph's pure delight.

To the Reverend THOMAS PERCY, D. D.

FROM claſſic plains, where ſcience loves to dwell,
Sooth'd with the warblings of her Attic ſhell ;
From bowers, where patriots, ſages, kings, have ſtray'd,
With wiſdom muſing in the laurel ſhade ;
Friend to the muſe, this votive verſe receive,
Praiſe what you can, and what you may, forgive.

Hither that muſe thy favour'd footſtep led,
And wreath'd a chaplet round thy youthful head :
Here bade thy ſoul, with daring ſearch, explore
The rich, exhauſtleſs mines of antient lore;
Reach the bold flights of Plato's fire-clad thought,
And ſcan the truths his greater maſter taught:
Wiſeſt of men, whoſe firm unſhaken ſoul
Beheld, without diſmay, the deadly bowl,
Nor cou'd ungrateful Athens blaſt a name,
That ſtill ſhall ſhine, their glory and their ſhame,
Here to thy view bade Athen's patriot riſe,
Fate in his voice, and light'ning in his eyes,

The

The foes of Greece and freedom to confound,
And dash the pride of Philip to the ground :
Or warm'd thee with the found of Tully's tongue,
On which admiring Rome with rapture hung,
Taught thee what ftrains the Theban roll'd along,
And all the fweets of Maro's polifh'd fong.

Oft, 'midft thefe kindred glades, thy mind might trace
The myftic page of Mona's antient race ;
Whom, trembling thro' her forefts inmoft gloom,
She pour'd by midnight from her cavern'd womb ;
Prophets, whofe eyes the depths of fate cou'd pierce,
Who burft the bands of death with magic verfe :
And thofe of later day, with rage fublime,
Who fmote the harp, and rouz'd the foul of rhyme ;
Whofe martial ftrains rehears'd the toils of fight,
And warm'd the heart of many a hardy knight :
How, like a rock, each lion-chieftain ftood,
Or urg'd his panting fteed thro' feas of hoftile blood.

Methinks I fee, where Alnwick's turrets hoar
Darken her flood, fo often ftain'd with gore,
A thoufand heroes fill the fpacious hall,
And helms and lances hang the frowning wall.

Full

Full in the center of the warlike band,

I fee a chief of bolder vifage ftand ;

With keener flames his glift'ning eye-balls fhine,

And his port marks him of the *Percy* line—

The fong begins; the minftrels fweep the ftring,

And the high roofs with martial clangors ring :

Of tournament they fing, and tented plain,

A Percy victor, or a Douglas flain,

Or Arthur's feats, in daring lays rehearfe,

Or Edward's conquefts fwell the mighty verfe;

The founds, like light'ning, pierce each warrior's foul,

And life's warm tides in brifker currents roll ;

Their fpears they fhake, and clafh the burnifh'd fhield,.

And feem triumphant e'er they reach the field—

    Bold were the notes, and kings approv'd the fong,

Like thofe who heard, unpolifh'd, rough, and ftrong ;

But cou'd not o'er the arm of death prevail,

When all the powers of fong and mufic fail :

Time, with oblivious hand, defac'd the page,

And virtue only triumph'd o'er his rage :

Their rugged numbers we no more admire,

Yet tho' their language fails, their raptures fire.

PERCY, 'twas thine to cull each nobler lay,.

And give new verdure to the wither'd bay ;.

The blooms of infant genius to reſtore,

Teach them to ſpread, and bid them fade no more—

For long as genuine paſſion ſways the heart,

And nature's painting ſhames the ſtrokes of art,

Britain ſhall love the ſtrain that ſings, ſo well,

How her bold antient heroes fought and fell :

Her riſing offspring kindle as they read,

And burn, like them, to conquer or to bleed—

To

To the AUTHOR of POEMS
And TRANSLATIONS from the Afiatic Languages.

WHITHER does fancy ftretch her rapid wing,
Thro' what new regions of ferener fpring ?
My ravifh'd fenfe an opening Eden greets,
A wafte of treafures, and a wild of fweets—
And now I feem thro' fairy bow'rs to ftray,
Where fcatter'd rubies pave the fpangled way;
Tranfparent walks, with polifh'd fapphires bright,
And * fountains, fparkling with ambrofial light.

A fweeter lyre no Eaftern fwain hath ftrung,
More foftly warbled, or more boldly fung;
Whether, great Bard, thy vigorous mufe rehearfe
Solima's deathlefs praife, in deathlefs verfe;
Paint the bright virtues of her generous mind,
Great as thy own, and as thy own refin'd;
Or, tun'd to grief, the melting numbers move,
And breathe the fofteft tales of plaintive love:

* Alluding to the poem of the Seven Fountains. See page 33.

C   Tender

Tender as Petrarch's flows th' impaſſion'd line,
Nor Vida boaſts a chaſter page than thine.

Yet not that Britain's laurels round thy head,
And Arab's palms with rival luſtre ſpread,
For this I ſing——but, that, with fix'd diſdain,
Thy Roman ſoul refus'd the flatterer's ſtrain;
And dar'd prefer, (unvers'd in courtly guile)
Virtue's juſt praiſe beyond a Monarch's ſmile.

To the Moſt Noble the MARQUIS of BLANDFORD,
after having ſeen Blenheim Houſe.

SUCH the proud monument of Churchill's fame,
Albion, thy boaſt, and vanquiſh'd Bourbon's ſhame;
Yet tho' the roofs, with ſtoried triumphs bright,
Pour on our eyes a flood of mimic light,
Tho' the rich walls, in breathing ſilks array'd,
Boaſt all the blended pomp of light and ſhade;
He claims a ſurer fame than theſe can give,
On nobler monuments his triumphs live:
For when this towering manſion ſhall decay,
(Forgive, great Architect, the daring lay)
When Time ſhall daſh to earth the mould'ring buſt,
And yon proud column crumbles into duſt,
In Britain's love his mem'ry ſtill ſhall bloom,
And anxious nations guard the warrior's tomb.

Here, BLANDFORD, oft, as to thy wond'ring eyes
His deathleſs feats in bright ſucceſſion riſe,
Congenial tranſports in thy boſom roll,
And half his ſpirit fires thy infant ſoul.

But

But far from thee the war's tumultuous rage,
Nor let ambition taint thy tender age;
Let Spencer's bright example teach thy mind
Sublimer joys, and tranfports more refin'd:
Like him, thy hand to pining want extend,
Protect the orphan, and the wretch befriend.
Thefe, thefe are arts that give more true renown,
Than captive nations, and a world o'erthrown.
But if thy country call thee to her caufe,
If freedom mourn her violated laws;
Then let thine arm the righteous fabre wield,
And be another Churchill in the field.

Yon lefs fuperb, yet not lefs glorious * pile,
Rear'd its fair front beneath his guardian fmile:
There, the pale victim of difeafe and grief,
Directs his feeble ftep, and finds relief:

* The Infirmary at Oxford, erected upon the moft extenfive and ufeful plan, by the Truftees of Dr. Radcliff's benefaction, out of the furplus money remaining after defraying the expences of his library, and fupported by the ample contributions of his Grace the Duke of Marlborough, and others of the nobility and gentry of Oxfordfhire. His Grace has likewife been a confiderable benefactor to the Univerfity, by prefenting it with an extenfive tract of ground for building an Obfervatory on, and with a reflecting telefcope of twelve feet, made by the late Mr. Short, which is the largeft inftrument of the kind ever made in England, (one only excepted, finifhed by the fame artift for the late King of Spain) and is of great value.

Defpair's

Defpair's wan cheeks the flufh of life refume,
And his pray'rs confecrate the hallow'd dome :
His grateful tongue of Radcliffe's bounty tells,
And on thy parent's name with rapture dwells.
The laurel'd fons of Ifis' happy vale
Catch the glad found, and fwell the applauding gale;
Her Naiads propagate the fav'rite theme,
And all her echoes waft it down the ftream.

But lo! attended by her infant train,
That fport around her on the velvet plain,
Like the firft blooming Eve, ere fatal pride
Led her fair feet from innocence afide,
The beauteous Marlbro' feeks her wonted fhade,
Where Perfian odours breathe thro' yonder glade;
Her fairer Paradife—for all the flowers
That fhed their foft perfumes in eaftern bowers,
Tranfplanted there their purple blooms expand,
And live and flourifh by her foft'ring hand.
But who are thefe, that flufh'd with all the glow
Which health and youthful beauty can beftow,
Amidft thofe fpicy fhrubs, themfelves more fweet,
Advance to meet her in her lov'd retreat?

In

In whom those charms, and ev'ry beauteous line
That marks her features, by reflection shine:
Our dazzled sight their rival splendors tire,
Nor know we which most justly to admire,
(So like they shine in ev'ry nobler grace)
The lovely parent, or her blooming race.

Hence let us haste to yonder rugged steep,
Down whose grey sides the plunging waters sweep;
Or climb yon mountain, black with hanging wood,
Round whose broad basis winds the deep'ning flood,
That, rolling thro' the spacious valley, shames,
With its proud waves, the meaner tide of Thames.
Such, Brown, the wonders of thy plastic hand;
The new creation sprang at thy command;
And yon stupendous arch surveys his tide
Astonish'd, spread with all an ocean's pride.

Beneath those elms, in Britain's elder time,
Old Chaucer pour'd his legendary rhyme:
To hear his wond'rous tales, the list'ning moon
Check'd her bright axle at its highest noon;
While many a wood-nymph round the bard would throng,
And dance responsive to his midnight song.

To

To thefe dear glooms, from battle's glorious toils,
With honours laden, and triumphal fpoils,
Great Henry fled *, to lofe in beauty's charms
The care of kingdoms, and the din of arms:
To rapture here, and Rofamond refign'd,
New paffions fir'd the royal Victor's mind :
The cleareft fprings they fought, the darkeft groves,
And ev'ry bower was confcious to their loves.
But fhort the blifs unholy joys afford,
His raging confort feeks her abfent lord ;
And Rofamond, from love and Henry torn,
Retires to weep in yonder glooms forlorn.
Oh never more may guilty tranfports ftain
Thefe hallow'd haunts, nor jealous fires profane ;
But ev'ry future lord, like Spenfer, prove
The fweets of focial life, and fpotlefs love !

* Henry the Second.

HERO

STRETCH'D on Abydos' folitary ftrand,
With eye erect to heav'n, and fuppliant hand,
Leander lay : the tempeft blacker grew,
And veil'd that heav'n for ever from his view !
He marks the boifterous hurricanes that fweep,
With madd'ning rage, the furface of the deep :
But fiercer ftorms within his bofom roll,
And furious gufts of paffion tear his foul.
Abfence and wild defpair at once confpire
To fwell the tumult, and inflame defire :
Sudden he ftarts, and thus, in frantic mood,
Pours his loud plaints to the remorfelefs flood.
" Thou reftlefs deep, whofe hoftile waves divide
" An eager lover, and his anxious bride,
" Ah ceafe thy rage ; ye tempefts rave no more,
" Nor bar my paffage to the wifh'd-for fhore :
" Much have I borne beneath your bleak domain,
" As each dark eve I crofs'd the watry plain.

" Raging

" Raging with fierce, impatient fires, to share

" The fond embraces of my abfent fair:

" Witnefs thou friendly torch, whofe glimmering light

" Chear'd the dull horrors of the dufky night;

" Witnefs ye confcious tow'rs, that oft have feen

" The trembling tranfports of your love-fick queen;

" When in her arms my dropping limbs fhe preft,

" And clafp'd me breathlefs, fainting to her breaft.

" Dear, tranfient fcenes! but ah! muft never more

" Thefe eyes with rapture view the Thracian fhore?

" Shall intervening feas, and adverfe wind,

" Damp or reftrain the lover's active mind?

" No, let me plunge amidft the foam, and brave

" All the wild fury of the dafhing wave:

" Soon on yon cliffs fhall blaze my well-known guide,

" While Hero's name fhall bear me thro' the tide.

" Fir'd at the found, my foul within me burns,

" And danger, toil and fate indignant fpurns."

He fpake, and rufhing down the rocky fteep,

Plung'd in the bofom of the hoary deep.

Now darknefs, brooding o'er the vaft profound,

Had fpread her dragon wing oe'r all around:

D

The

The pale moon funk amidft the tenfold night,
And ev'ry ftar with-held its chearing light:
Defcending torrents, mix'd with ruddy flame,
Roar'd to the howling blaft in loud acclaim;
The pealing thunders broke thro' heav'n's cleft plain,
And fhook the caverns of the groaning main;
Nor ceas'd the lightnings, with deftructive glare,
To flafh impetuous thro' the dufky air.
Leander, frantic with amaze and dread,
Amidft the billows rear'd his languid head,
And fought the faithful lamp, but none appear'd,
And not a ray the dark horizon chear'd,
Save where the lightning fhot a dreadful gleam,
Or fparkles gliften'd on the glowing ftream.
In vain to heav'n he lifts his haggard eyes,
Adds vow to vow, and wearies Jove with cries:
No pitying God would grant a lover's pray'r,
Nor Venus hear his wailings of defpair.
He next invokes old Neptune to his aid,
And ev'ry nymph, and ev'ry blue-ey'd maid,
In vain; relentlefs fate had feal'd his doom;
The deep, to whelm him, opes her yawning womb.

Exhaufted

Exhaufted with fatigue, at length he gave
His languid limbs to float along the wave;
Then, heaving from his breaft a mighty figh,
Exclaim'd, " 'Tis heaven's decree, and I muft die:
" Muft die, my Hero, ere thefe circling arms
" Once more, in thine, embrace an angel's charms.
" Ye cruel winds, ye fportive tempefts, hear
" Thefe my laft words, and waft them to my dear.
" Tell her, not all your rage combin'd could move
" This conftant foul, nor quench the fire of love:
" Tell her, for her I brav'd the boift'rous tide,
" For her the madnefs of the ftorm—and died."
He faid; and darknefs rufhing on his fight,
Wrapt the pale lover in eternal night.

Hero meanwhile, with anxious cares oppreft,
A thoufand paffions ftruggling in her breaft,
Pafs'd in fufpenfe her tedious hours away,
The night in watching, and in tears the day.
Now, from the higheft tow'r fhe ftretch'd, with pain,
Her eager eyes o'er all the boundlefs main;
Now with her flaves from room to room fhe flies,
Till the wide dome refounded with their cries.

At

At length she paus'd, her strength began to fail,
And thus she spake, with faultering lips and pale—

　" Dear partners of my grief, who m re than share
" In all the complicated pangs I bear,
" Did ever wretch such various tortures know,
" Toil with like cares, or bend with equal woe?
" I sink, I sink beneath the mighty weight,
" And yield me to the torrent of my fate—
" Thrice hath the moon her nightly journey roll'd,
" Nor yet these arms the lovely youth infold;
" Perhaps, already, welt'ring on the wave,
" O'er his pale head the circling billows rave.
" Hah there!—I see him mangled, gash'd, and torn,
" Wide o'er the howling waste of waters borne.
" I see him dash'd against the rocky shore,
" His beauteous limbs all black with wounds and gore:
" Help, help, ye powers!"——the fainting princess said,
And her slaves bear her to the royal bed.

　In vain she strove her languid eye to close,
And lose the sense of grief in sweet repose,
Such dreadful scenes within her bosom wrought,
And doubt and terror darken ev'ry thought:.

Before

Before her fight the ghaftly phantom ftood,
All deadly pale, and fmear'd with clotted blood;
Dreadful it fmil'd, as o'er her proftrate charms
It feem'd to hang, and ftretch its empty arms.
The gloomy vifion fir'd her madd'ning brain,
And wilder horror fhot thro' ev'ry vein.
She ftarted from the couch in wild defpair,
Beat her white breaft and tore her raven hair;
Then, rufhing forth, the rocky heights afcends,
Where wideft o'er the wave the turret bends;
Rolling her fiery eyes from fide to fide,
Soon as her lover's floating corpfe fhe fpied,
Headlong fhe darted from the giddy fteep,
And funk for ever in the whelming deep.

HIND A.

LED by the ftar of evening's guiding fires,
That fhone ferene on Aden's lofty fpires,
Young Agib trod the folitary plain,
Where groves of fpikenard greet his fenfe in vain :
In wealth o'er all the neighbouring fwains fupreme,
For manly beauty ev'ry virgin's theme;
But no repofe his anxious bofom found,
Where forrow cherifh'd an eternal wound.
The frequent figh, wan look, and frantic ftart,
Spoke the defpair that prey'd upon his heart.
The haunts of men no more his fteps invite,
Nor India's treafures give his foul delight.
In fields and deep'ning fhades he fought relief,
And thus difcharg'd the torrent of his grief.

' Ye fwains, that thro' the bow'rs of pleafure rove,
' Ye nymphs, that range the myrtle glades of love,
' Forgive a wretch, whofe feet your bow'rs prophane,
' Where joy alone and happy lovers reign :

' But oh! this breaſt inceſſant cares corrode,

' And urge my fainting ſteps to death's abode!

' Joyleſs to me the ſeaſons roll away,

—' Exhauſted nature hurries to decay;

' Day's chearful beams for me in vain return,

' For me the ſtars of heav'n neglected burn:

' In vain the flow'rs in wild luxuriance blow,

' In vain the fruits with purple radiance glow;

' In vain the harveſt groans, the vintage bleeds,

' Grief urges grief, and toil to toil ſucceeds:

' Since ſhe whoſe preſence bade the world be gay,

' Whoſe charms gave luſtre to the brighteſt day,

' H I N D A, once faireſt of the virgin train,

' Who haunt the foreſt, or who range the plain,

' Sleeps where the boughs of yon black cypreſs wave,

' And I am left to languiſh at her grave!

' To that dear ſpot, when day's declining beam

' Darts from yon ſhining towers a farewell gleam,

' Conſtant as eve, my ſorrows I renew,

' And mix my tears with the deſcending dew,

' The laſt ſad debt to buried beauty pay,

' Kiſs the cold ſhrine, and claſp the mould'ring clay.

I.   ' Far.

' Far other founds this confcious valley heard,

' Far other vows thefe ardent lips preferr'd,

' When fick with love, and eager to embrace

' Beauties unrivall'd but by angel grace,

' I madden'd as I gaz'd o'er all her charms,

' And hail'd my HINDA to a bridegroom's arms.

' I printed on her lips an hafty kifs,

' The pledge of ardent love and future blifs;

' Her glowing blufhes fann'd the fecret fire,

' Gave life to love, and vigour to defire;

' Then, when the tear, warm trickling down my cheek,

' Spoke the full language paffion could not fpeak,

' Our mutual tranfport feal'd the nuptial rite,

' Heav'n witnefs'd, and approv'd the chafte delight——

" Prepare, I cried, prepare the nuptial feaft,

" Bring all the treafures of the rifled Eaft:

" The choiceft gifts of ev'ry clime explore,

" Let * Aden yield her tributary ftore;

---

* Aden and Saba are both cities of Arabia Felix, celebrated for the gardens and fpicy woods with which they are furrounded.

" Let

" Let Saba all her beds of spice unfold,

" And Samarcand send gems, and India gold,

" To deck a banquet worthy of the bride,

" Where mirth shall be the guest, and love preside.

" Full fifty steeds I boast of swiftest pace,

" Fierce in the fight, and foremost in the race.'

" Slaves too I have, a numerous, faithful band,

" And heav'n hath giv'n me wealth with lavish hand :

" Yet never have I heap'd an useless store,

" Nor spurn'd the needy pilgrim from my door;

" And, skill'd alike to wield the crook or sword,

" I scorn the mandate of the proudest lord.

" O'er my wide vales a thousand camels bound,

" A thousand sheep my fertile hills surround;

" For her amidst the spicy shrubs they feed,

" For her the choicest of the flock shall bleed :

" Of polish'd chrystal shall a goblet shine,

" The surface mantling with the richest wine;

" And on its sides with * Omman's pearls inlaid,

" Full many a tale of love shall be pourtray'd :

---

* The sea of Omman bounds Arabia on the south, and is celebrated by the Eastern Poets for the beauty of the pearls it produces.

E

" Hesper

" Hefper fhall rife and warn us to be gone,

" Yet will we revel 'till the breaking dawn;

" Nor will we heed the morn's unwelcome light,

" Nor our joys finifh with returning night.

" Not Georgia's nymphs can with my love compare,

" Like jet, the ringlets of her mufky hair:

" Her ftature like the palm, her fhape the pine,

" Her breafts like fwelling clufters of the vine;

" Fragrant her breath as Hadramut's perfume,

" And her cheeks fhame the damafk rofe's bloom.

" Black, foft, and full, her eyes ferenely roll,

" And feem the liquid manfion of her foul.

" Who fhall defcribe her lips, where rubies glow,

" Her teeth like fhining drops of pureft fnow?

" Beneath her honey'd tongue perfuafion lies,

" And her voice breathes the ftrains of Paradife.

" A bower I have, where branching almonds fpread,

" Where all the feafons all their bounties fhed;

" The gales of life amidft the branches play,

" And mufic burfts from ev'ry vocal fpray,

" Its verdant foot a ftream of amber laves,

" And o'er it Love his guardian banner waves:

' There

" There fhall our days, our nights in pleafure glide,

" Friendfhip fhall live when paffion's joys fubfide;

" Increafing years improve our mutual truth,

' And age give fanction to the choice of youth."

' Thus fondly I of fancied raptures fung,

' And with my fong the gladden'd valley rung.

' But fate, with jealous eye, beheld our joy,

' Smil'd to deceive, and flatter'd to deftroy;

' Swift as the fhades of night the vifion fled,

' Grief was the gueft, and death the banquet fpread.

' A burning fever on her vitals prey'd,

' Defied Love's efforts, baffled med'cine's aid,

' And from thefe widow'd arms a treafure tore,

' Beyond the price of empires to reftore.

' What have I left, what portion but defpair,

' Long days of woe, and nights of endlefs care?

' While others live to love, I live to weep;

' Will forrow burft the grave's eternal fleep?

' Will all my pray'rs the favage tyrant move

' To quit his prey, and give me back my love?

' If far, far hence, I take my hafty flight,

' Seek other haunts, and fcenes of foft delight,

' Amidft

' Amidſt the crouded mart her voice I hear,

' And ſhed, unſeen, the ſolitary tear;

' Muſic exalts her animating ſtrain,

' And beauty rolls her radiant eye in vain :

' All that was muſic fled with Hinda's breath,

' And beauty's brighteſt eyes are clos'd in death !

' I pine in darkneſs for the ſolar rays,

' Yet loath the ſun, and ſicken at his blaze;

' Then curſe the light, and curſe the lonely gloom,

' While unremitting ſorrow points the tomb.

' Oh ! Hinda, brighteſt of the black-ey'd maids,

' That ſport in paradiſe' embow'ring ſhades,

' From golden boughs where bend ambroſial fruits,

' And fragrant waters waſh th' immortal roots ;

' Oh from the bright abodes of purer day,

' The proſtrate Agib at thy tomb ſurvey ;

' Behold me with unceaſing vigils pine,

' My youthful vigour waſte with ſwift decline ;

' My hollow eye behold, and faded face,

' Where health but lately ſpread her ruddy grace—

' I can no more—this ſabre ſets me free ;

' This gives me back to rapture, love and thee.

' Firm

' Firm to the ftroke its fhining edge I bare,

' The lover's laft fad folace in defpair.

' Go, faithful fleel, act ling'ring nature's part,

' Bury thy blufhing point within my heart;

' Drink all the life that warms thefe drooping veins,

' And banifh at one ftroke a thoufand pains.

' Hafte thee, dear charmer; catch my gafping breath,

' And chear with fmiles the barren glooms of death!

' 'Tis done—the gates of Paradife expand—

' Attendant Houri feize my trembling hand—

' I pafs the dark, inhofpitable fhore,

' And, Hinda, thou art mine—to part no more.'

THE

THE PROSPECT OF LIFE:

AN ODE.

THOU, in whofe breaft ambitious tranfports burn,
   And ye, who wafte the vigour of your age
In fruitlefs wifhes to protract the date,
Affign'd to life by unrelenting fate ;
Ah from the fcenes of fplendid folly turn,
   And mark her mirror in this faithful page.

What tho', blind wretch, along her dang'rous tide,
Sportive, the thoughtlefs and the giddy glide ;
   Or, led by folly's meteor light aftray,
Securely wanton round the verdant fhore :
   How are they fwept by fudden fates away,
Or break like bubbles and are heard no more !

                                 But

But if thou wilt the untried ocean dare,

For rougher ſtorms thy ſhatter'd bark prepare,

 When all thy boaſted ſkill ſhall fail;

For many a rock lurks unperceiv'd beneath,

And know,—creation teems with various death,

 With ſecret treaſures of exhauſtleſs woe,

 That o'er the deareſt joys of man prevail,

And cruſh the happineſs of all below.

Behold the circling elements conſpire

 To hurry hapleſs mortals to the tomb,

Leagued to deſtroy, earth, ocean, air, and fire,

 With active violence urge on their doom.

 Deeply convuls'd with thunder's awful ſound,

See the cleft earth diſcloſe her yawning womb,

 And whelm whole empires in the gulph profound !

 Eruptive thro' the midnight air

Fell comets flaſh, and vivid lightnings glare,

Smiting with death the guiltleſs victim's head,

Or ruſhing whirlwinds deſolate the plain,

 Where Afric's barren waſte expands,

And caravans, with nations in their train,

 Promiſcuous bury in the burning ſands.

3

But who shall ocean's countless wrecks rehearse,

The myriads welt'ring on her stormy bed?

    Stupendous tomb of half the human race,

That sleep unwept by one funereal verse,

    One mournful tear their obsequies to grace!

From scenes of public terror turn thy view;

Fate's thousand ills in humbler scenes pursue:

Extend thy glance thro' ev'ry various stage,

From childhood's follies up to doating age—

What then is life, but one vast chearless maze,

    Where blinded man in error strays;

    Alternate sport of joy and sorrow,

To-day triumphant, and oppres'd to-morrow?

    First let thine eye attentive scan

    What nameless woes thy steps await,

Ere ripening years mature thee into man,

And darken ev'ry prospect of delight:

    Scarce has the frail inhabitant of clay,

'Midst toil and danger, struggled into day;

    But infant screams too well declare

The wretched babe misfortune's fated heir.

                         Perhaps

Perhaps he falls her early prey,
　　And finks untimely to the grave;
But if his tender head her fury brave,
　　And fate this happieſt boon deny,
　　A thouſand furies hover nigh,
In haſt'ning years, their certain prey to ſeize:
A thouſand ravening paſſions ready ſtand,
Each with a whip of ſcorpions in his hand;
Theſe, with united rage, his boſom ſting,
　　Blaſt all his hopes, and poiſon ev'ry ſpring
Whence genuine rapture had begun to flow,
　　And ſpread an univerſal blank of woe!
While unaſſuag'd and piercing pains,
　　The monſtrous race of peſtilent diſeaſe,
Infuriate ruſh thro' all his throbbing veins,
　　To madneſs ev'ry frantic pulſe inflame,
And writhe with agony his tortur'd frame.
　　Then viſionary fears his ſoul affright;
　　He finks in fuperſtition's tenfold night.

　　Now let the muſe exalt her ſtrain;
Let martial clangors drown the voice of pain:
Behold him, now, in life's meridian ſtate,
　　When all the ſyren pleaſures round him wait;

F　　　　　　　　　　　　　　His

His cheeks with health and manly beauty glow,
And valour frowns upon his dauntlefs brow :
    What tho', inflam'd with glory's charms,
He rufhes at the trumpet's call to arms,
And gains the fhining plume of high renown ?
    Perhaps, the loftieft fummit gain'd,
With ev'ry bold, ambitious wifh obtain'd,
    He triumphs in his foes o'erthrown,
And boafts the fplendors of a ravifh'd crown :
    Yet foon the glittering phantom flies,
    The widow's moan hath pierc'd the fkies :
Some frefh ufurper rifes to confound
    His tow'ring pride ; and fortune's changeful frown
Tumbles the victim of her vengeance down.

    But thus to triumph, thus to fall,
Is not the guilty, glorious lot of all :
    Yet ev'ry breaft with various paffion burns,
And the fad profpect ftill thro' life returns.
    Does fcience court thee ? ah the wifh forego,
For added knowledge is but added woe ;
    Error and doubt diftract the fchoolman's mind,
Happier, tho' humbler, refts th' untutor'd hind.

                          ·   In

In senfual joys you plunge, but plunge in vain,
No heartfelt pleafures are to thefe allied;
   The feftive board unfeen difeafes ftain,
And forrow floats amidft the crimfon tide.

   Does beauty fire thee? know, that ficklieft fiow'r
Blooms and expires, the product of an hour!
   Bright, but to perifh; blooming, but to fade;
The lovelieft cheek that ever wak'd defire,
   The brighteft eye muft foon its charms refign;
Refign at once their luftre and their fire,
   And hide their glories in eternal fhade!

But fay, do bafer tranfports warm thy foul,
   Ambitious ftill to fwell thy fhining ftore,
And, mines exhaufted, yet athirft for more?
   Take then the utmoft wifh that foul can frame;
For thee, her treafures let Pactolus roll,
   For thee, the diamonds of Golconda flame:
Yet Oh! when death fhall lift the threaten'd dart,
   When keen remorfe, for all the victims flain
To fatiate thy unbounded thirft for gain,
   Plunges her fiery talon in thy heart;

                             Will

Will thefe remorfelefs Proferpine affuage,
Will thefe allay the bofom fury's rage?

Ah! why the catalogue of ills prolong,
And fwell with complicated woes the fong?
Recount thofe darker moments of defpair,
 When all the paffions, fierce and unconfin'd,
 Rufh with the tempeft's fury on the mind,
And reafon, headlong, from her ftation bear:
When poverty to ev'ry other pang
 Adds her keen edge—prefents an infant train,
 Who with imploring eyes around thee hang,
And raife their fuppliant plaints for bread in vain:
Stern fate, perhaps, determin'd to deftroy
 All that was precious, all thou wifh'd to fave,
And crufh at once the fource of ev'ry joy—
Blafts the young confort blooming in thy arms;
Nips in the bud a daughter's op'ning charms,
 Or gives thy bofom friend to an untimely grave.

Then, ev'ry fource of genuine comfort dead,
Youth's fire extinct, and manhood's vigour fled,
 To clofe the dreary fcene, enfeebling age,
With fault'ring foot, and furrow'd front appears,

Jealous,

Jealous, miſtruſtful, impotent; oppreſs'd
With never-ceaſing doubts and groundleſs fears,
   Without one hope to warm the languid breaſt,
Thy toil to ſoften, or thy grief aſſuage.
The pow'rs of memory fail; the balls of ſight,
   " With dim ſuffuſion veil'd," no more retain
Their ſparkling beams, but ſhed a doubtful light.
No more the deafen'd ears can drink the ſound
   Of plaintive lute, or ſoftly-warbling lyre:
The nervous arms no longer dart around
   The brandiſh'd javelin, or avenging fire.
Fall'n is their boaſted might, and nought remains
   As life's laſt remnant moments tedious flow,
   But black reſerves of unexhauſted pains,
And ſad ſucceſſive ſcenes of length'ning woe!

VERSES

" WHAT shouts were those; what fierce and martial train
" Rushes to war in yon embattled plain?
" Ah whence those flames that brighten all the coast,
" And light to vengeance each devoted host?
" Oh! scene of guilt, that blots the sick'ning day!
" And must a parent's eyes that scene survey?
" My sons, my sons, in impious fight engage,
" And brothers madden with forbidden rage."
Thus from the bosom of th' Atlantic tide,
While at her voice th' obsequious waves divide,
Slow-rising, Britain's guardian Genius said;
And tore th' eternal laurels from her head.
Her foot she fix'd upon the rocky steep,
Where * Boston's barrier cliffs o'erhang the deep:
In vain she stretch'd her anxious eyes around,
To the broad horizon's remotest bound;

---

* These rocks are at the entrance of the bay, and are so many and dangerous as to allow only one safe approach to the harbour, through a channel hardly wide enough to admit two ships to sail in abreast.

The

The fmiling fields, the peopled marts to trace
The happy haunts of her once favour'd race.
Thofe fields, thofe marts, were now a defart grown,
Their beauty vanifh'd, and their pride o'erthrown.
Inftant the warrior flufh, that wont to ftreak
With glowing crimfon her immortal cheek,
Exchang'd for deadly pale its radiant dies,
And the keen lightnings languifh'd in her eyes;
The fhield of glory trembled in her hand,
Her fpear fhe dafh'd upon the ftony ftrand:
And as fhe view'd the defolated plain,
Pour'd from her burfting heart this plaintive ftrain.

" Ah, fatal fields! where, erft the chofen band,
" Fir'd by my voice, and led by freedom's hand,
" Thro' wild untrodden defarts burft their way,
" Where yelling favages in ambufh play;
" Where the grim wolf lay dormant in the brake,
" And vengeance fparkled from the trampled fnake—
" Ah race unworthy thofe immortal fires,
" Debas'd their virtues, tho' not quench'd their fires,
" Ye, who thofe fpears with brother's blood have ftain'd;
" What nights of toil and days of battle gain'd,

" To

" To murd'rous difcord have refign'd a prey;

" And marr'd the toil of ages in a day.

" Dar'd they, for this, the polar winter's fnow;

" For this, the burning fun's intenfer glow?

" For this did many a hero ftrew the plain,

" When * Potowmack ran purple to the main?

" For this, my Wolfe his life victorious pour,

" And Braddock perifh on a barb'rous fhore?

" Behold, my fons, this wounded breaft I bare,

" Ah ceafe thefe ftreaming wounds afrefh to tear!

" From you they came; and ev'ry hoftile dart

" Drinks my warm life, and rankles at my heart.

" Sheathe, fheathe your fwords; or, if the rage of fight

" Fill my bold race with fuch fevere delight,

" (For well I know what martial ardors roll

" In breafts like yours, and fire the warrior foul)

" Hafte to the fields where fairer glory calls;

" Hafte, hurl your thunder round Havannah's walls.

" Once more infulting Spain fhall flee with dread,

" And haughty Bourbon bow the ftubborn head.

---

* Potowmack is a confiderable river of Virginia, where the firft fettlers eftablifhed their colony, after furmounting every obftacle of an unknown country and a favage enemy.

Infpir'd

" Infpir'd with dark revenge, and rival hate,

" They plan deftruction for my fav'rite ftate :

" Eager to crufh a pow'r, their fcourge and fhame,

" With hell's dire arts your difcords they inflame ;

" 'Till civil torches light them on their way,

" And hofts refiftlefs feize th' unguarded prey.

" But fhall my Britons, whofe exalted name

" Shines on the bright record of nobler fame ;

" Shall the bold fons of freedom and the waves,

" Shrink at the nod of Gaul's imperious flaves ?

" A race for treacherous arts alone renown'd,.

" Who know of honour nothing fave the found ;

" But vers'd in flatt'ry, and grimace, and guile,

" Betray with bows, and murder with a fmile :

" Shall thefe rule Britons ? Firft, ye lightnings, fweep

" Thefe blafted cliffs, and whelm them in the deep.

" What tho' no foft luxurious arts ye boaft,

" Rough like your native clime, and rugged coaft,

" Ye glory in the nobler arts of truth,

" And manlier paffions fire your vig'rous youth ;

" Courage is theirs, and noble thirft of fame,

" Virtue's ftrong throb, and honour's virgin flame :

G   " Thefe

" Thefe are your bulwark, and when thefe fhall fall,

" Britons fhall crouch the abject flaves of Gaul.

" Have ye forgotten Creffy's glorious field,

" Where my lov'd Henry rais'd the warrior fhield;

" Where glory's felf his victor armies led,

" And with three crowns adorn'd his royal head?

" Before him fee her glittering ftandard borne,

" Her laurels blafted, and her lilies torn;

" See at bis feet her captive monarch bow,

" And wail the jewels ravifh'd from his brow.

" Rouze, let rekindling fancy call to view

" The coward heaps immortal Marlbro' flew;

" His arm but rais'd, oppofing hofts retire,

" Or feek in death a refuge from his ire.

" Methinks I fee a train of heroes rife,

" Flames in their hands, and terrors in their eyes;

" Revenge!" they fhout, and tow'rds Havannah's fpires

" Wave their red arms, and point their hoftile fires.

" Rouze then, my fons, nor heed the fullen roar,

" Which jealous faction yells around your fhore:

" Soon fhall the hydra fpend her pois'nous breath,

" By me dragg'd howling to the gates of death.

Once

" Once more, in arms united as in mind,

" Be firm, and brave the powers of earth combin'd :

" Gallia ſhall ſhrink aghaſt, and vaunting Spain

" Strive with the miſtreſs of the world in vain."

She ſpake ; the luſtre to her eye return'd,
Her cheek with renovated crimſon burn'd ;
Eager ſhe graſp'd th' unconquerable blade,
And all the terrors of her ſhield diſplay'd :
Then ſwiftly plung'd in Ocean's mighty bed,
And the bright billows ſparkled o'er her head..

VERSES

VERSES intended as a PROLOGUE
To the TRACHINIANS of SOPHOCLES,

Performed by the Scholars of the Rev. Mr. PARR, at Stanmore
in Middlesex.

THE son of Jove, with anxious qualms oppress'd,
To soothe the manes of his murder'd guest,
In willing exile roves to distant climes:
Strange doctrines these to rogues of modern times;
Whom scarce stern justice can expel the land,
Tho' steady Mansfield guide her vengeful hand.
But what you'll think more strange, he takes his wife,
To swell the sorrows of his future life.
As on they journey, silent, pensive, slow,
Hearts full of grief, and eyes that stream with woe,
A river stopp'd their course—ye powers divine !
How could you thwart so pious a design ?
The Hero paus'd, the Lady gave a scream,
At length appear'd the genius of the stream :
A huge misshapen clown, with face of brass,
That well might for an Irish porter pass :
Nx-Nx-Nxxx,—I think—confound the barb'rous name,
Like Hercules himself in strength and fame,
Across his shoulders our fair heroine strode,
And thus in triumph thro' the billows rode.

One

One would have thought the waters might affuage
The monfter's heat, and cool his brutifh rage;
But fpite of all, this huge, this ill-form'd wight,
Dar'd utter words, fo rude and unpolite——
Dar'd offer things—fo fhocking to be told,
As made the prudifh lady's blood run cold——
To fuch a height increas'd his vile defire,
It rouz'd the watchful hufband's jealous ire,
Who, inftant as he reach'd th' oppofing fhore,
Hurl'd the fwift arrow, dipt in pois'nous gore,
That ftopp'd the faithlefs mifcreant in his flight,
And fent him howling to the fhades of night!
But ere the laft pang heav'd his ftubborn breaft,
With rage, with anguifh, and revenge opprefs'd,
The Centaur thus the trembling dame addrefs'd:
" If e'er thy hufband wander from thy arms,
" Or gaze with fondnefs on another's charms;
" This veftment fprinkled with my blood, fhall prove
" A pow'rful charm, and bind him to thy love."

Sage counfel; which our Heroine did not fail
To ponder well, as mortal flefh is frail——
Time prov'd her right; for foon this conftant lord,
So fond, fo true, a neighb'ring nymph ador'd;

And

And while conflicting paſſions tear her breaſt,
She ſends her faithleſs ſpouſe this fatal veſt :
The envenom'd robe his tortur'd ſinews fires,
And the falſe wretch in dreadful pangs expires.

Ladies, i'faith, theſe Grecian dames, I ween,
Were full of ranc'rous ſpite, and deadly ſpleen ;
Our Britiſh nymphs, of yore, were ſomewhat cruel,
And ſlew their rival ſweethearts in a duel:
But you, fair virgins, more polite and wiſe,
Contented *murder* mortals, *with your eyes.*
And, if neglectful of his ſpouſe at home,
In theſe our days a huſband chance to roam;
The prudent wife ſuch wanton vengeance ſcorns,.
And decks his temples—with a brace of horns.

THE SCHOOL-BOY.

In the Manner of the Splendid Shilling.

THRICE happy he, whofe hours the chearing fmiles
Of freedom blefs; who wantons uncontroul'd
Where eafe invites, or pleafure's fyren voice;
Him the ftern tyrant with his iron fcourge
Annoys not, nor the dire oppreffive weight
Of galling chain; but when the blufhing morn
Purples the eaft, with eager tranfport wild,
O'er hill, o'er valley, on his panting fteed
He bounds exulting, as in full career
With horns, and hounds, and thund'ring fhouts he drives
The flying ftag; or when the dufky fhades
Of eve, advancing veil the darkened fky,
To neighb'ring tavern, blithfome, he reforts
With boon companion, where they drown their cares
In fprightly bumpers, and the mantling bowl.

Far otherwife within thefe darkfome walls,
Whofe gates, with rows of triple fteel fecur'd,
And many a bolt, prohibit all egrefs,
I fpend my joylefs days; ere dawn appears,

Rous'd

Rous'd from my peaceful ſlumbers by the ſound
Of awe-inſpiring bell, whoſe every ſtroke
Chills my heart-blood, all trembling, I deſcend
From dreary garret, round whoſe ancient roof,
Gaping with hideous chinks, the whiſtling blaſt
Perpetual raves, and fierce deſcending rains
Diſcharge their fury—Dire, lethargic dews
Oppreſs my drowſy ſenſe; ſtill fancy teems
With fond, ideal joys, and, fil'd with what
Or Poets ſing, or fabled tale records,
Preſents tranſporting viſions; goblets crown'd
With juice of Nectar, or the food divine
Of rich Ambroſia, tempting to the ſight!
While in the ſhade of ſome embow'ring grove
I lie reclin'd, or through Elyſian plains
Enraptur'd ſtray; where ev'ry plant and flower
Send forth an odorous ſmell, and all the air
With ſongs of love and melody reſounds.
Meanwhile benumbing cold invades my joints,
As with ſlow fault'ring footſteps I reſort
To where, of antique mold, a lofty dome
Rears its tremendous front; here all at once
From thouſand different tongues, a mighty hum
Aſſaults my ears; loud as the diſtant roar

Of

Of tumbling torrents ; or as in fome mart
Of public note, for traffic far renown'd,
Where Jew with Grecian, Turk with African,
Affembled, in one general peal unite
Of dreadful jargon.—Strait on wooden bench
I take my feat, and conn with ftudious care
Th' appointed tafks ; o'er many a puzzling page
Poring intent, and fage Athenian bard,
With dialect, and mood and tenfe perplex'd ;
And conjugations varied without end.

When lo ! with haughty ftride (in fize like him
Who erft extended on the burning lake,
Lay floating many a rood ;) his fullen brow,
With low'ring frowns and fearful glooms o'ercaft,
Enters the Pædagogue ; terrific fight !
An ample ninefold peruke, fpread immenfe,
Luxuriant waving down his fhoulders plays ;
His hand a bunch of limber twigs fuftains,
Call'd by the vulgar Birch, tartarean root,
Whofe rankling points, in blackeft poifon dipt,
Inflict a mortal pain ; and, where they light,
A ghaftly furrow leave.—Scar'd at the fight,

H

'The

The buſtling multitude, with anxious hearts,
Their ſtations ſeek.----A ſolemn pauſe enſues;
As when, of old, the monarch of the floods,
'Midſt raging hurricanes, and battling waves,
Shaking the dreadful Trident, rear'd aloft
His awful brow.---Sudden the furious winds
Were huſh'd in peace, the billows ceas'd their rage:
Or when, (if mighty themes, like theſe, allow
An humble metaphor) the ſportive race
Of nibbling heroes, bent on wanton play,
Beneath the ſhelter of ſome well-ſtor'd barn,
In many an airy circle wheel around;
Some eye, perchance, in private nook conceal'd,
Beholds GRIMALKIN; inſtant they diſperſe,
In headlong flight, each to his ſecret cell;
If haply he may 'ſcape impending fate.

Thus ceas'd the gen'ral clamour; all remain
In ſilent terror wrapt, and thought profound.

Meanwhile, the Pædagogue throughout the dome.
His fiery eyeballs, like two blazing ſtars,
Portentous rolls, on ſome unthinking wretch,
To ſhed their baleful influence; whilſt his voice
Like thunder, or the cannon's ſudden burſt,

Three

Three times is heard, and thrice the roofs refound !
A fudden palenefs gathers in my face ;
Through all my limbs a ftiff'ning horror fpreads,
Cold as the dews of death, nor heed my eyes
Their wonted function, but in ftupid gaze
Ken the fell monfter; from my trembling hands
The thumb-worn volume drops ; oh dire prefage
Of inftant woe! for now the mighty found
Pregnant with difmal tidings, once again
Strikes my aftonifh'd ears.   Transfix'd with awe,
And fenfelefs, for a time, I ftand; but foon,
By friendly jog, or neighb'ring whifper rous'd,
Obey the dire injunction ; ftrait I loofe
Depending brogues, and mount the lofty throne
Indignant, or the back oblique afcend
Of forrowful compeer; nor long delays
The Monarch, from his palace ftalking down,
With vifage all inflam'd ; his fable robe
Sweeping in length'ning folds along the ground :
He fhakes his fceptre, and the impending fcourge
Brandifhes high ; nor tears nor fhrieks avail;
But with impetuous fury it defcends,
Imprinting horrid wounds, with fatal flow
Of blood attended, and convulfive pangs.

Curft

Curst be the wretch, for ever doom'd to bear
Infernal whippings; he, whose savage hands
First grasp'd these barbarous weapons, bitter cause
Of foul disgrace, and many a dolorous groan,
To hapless school-boy.—Could it not suffice
I groan'd and toil'd beneath the merc'less weight,
By stern relentless tyranny impos'd,
But scourges too, and cudgels were reserv'd
To goad my harrow'd sides : This wretched life
Loading with heavier ills; a life expos'd
To all the woes of hunger, toil, distress ;
Cut off from ev'ry genial source of bliss;
From ev'ry bland amusement, wont to soothe
The youthful breast ; except when father Time,
In joyful change, rolls round the festive hour,
That gives this meagre, pining figure, back
To parent fondness, and its native roofs.
Fir'd with the thought, then, then my tow'ring soul
Rises superior to its load, and spurns
Its proud oppressors ; frantic with delight,
My fancy riots in successive scenes
Of bliss and pleasures : plans and schemes are laid
How best the fleeting moments to improve,
Nor lose one portion of so rare a boon.

3

But foon, too foon, thefe glorious fcenes are fled,
Scarce one fhort moon enjoy'd, (oh ! tranfient ftate
Of fublunary blifs) by bitter change,
And other fcenes fucceeded, what fierce pangs
Then rack my foul ; what ceafelefs floods of grief,
Rufh down my cheeks, while ftrong convulfive throbs
Heave all my frame, and choak the power of fpeech.
Forlorn I figh, nor heed the gentle voice
Of friend or ftranger, who, with foothing words,
And flender gift, would fain beguile my woes ;·
In vain ; for what can aught avail to foothe
Such raging anguifh ! Oft with fudden glance
Before my eyes in all its horrors glares
That well-known form, and oft I feem to hear
The thund'ring fcourge—Ah me ! e'en now I feel
Its deadly venom, raging as the pangs
That tore Alcides, when the burning veft
Prey'd on his wafted fides.—At length return'd
Within thefe hated walls, again I mourn
A fullen pris'ner, 'till the wifh'd approach
Of joyous holiday or feftive play
Releafes me : ah ! freedom that muft end
With thee, declining Sol ; all hail, ye fires
For fanctity renown'd, whofe glorious names

In

In large confpicuous charaƈters pourtray'd,
Adorn the annual chronologic page
Of Wing or Partridge; oft when fore opprefĭ
With dire calamities, the glad return
Of your triumphant feĭtivals, hath chear'd
My drooping foul; nor be thy name forgot,
Illuĭtrious George, for much to thee I owe
Of heart-felt rapture, as with loyal zeal
Glowing, I pile the crackling bonfire high,
Or hurl the mounting rocket thro' the air,
Or fiery whizzing ferpent; thus thy name
Shall ĭtill be honour'd, as thro' future years
The circling feafons roll their feĭtive round.

Sometimes, by dire compulfive hunger prefs'd,
I fpring the neighb'ring fence, and fcale the trunk
Of apple-tree; or wide, o'er flow'ry lawns,
By hedge ɔ thicket, bend my haĭty ĭteps,
Intent, with fecret ambuĭh, to furprize
The ĭtraw-built neĭt, and unfufpeƈting brood
Of Thruĭh or Bullfinch; oft with watchful ken
Eyeing the backward lawns, leĭt hoĭtile glance
Obferve my footĭteps, while each ruĭtling leaf,
Stirr'd by the gentle gale, alarms my fears:

Then,

Then, parch'd beneath the burning heats of noon,

I plunge into the limpid stream, that laves

The silent vale, or on its grassy banks

Beneath some oak's majestic shade, recline;

Envying the vagrant fishes, as they pass

Their boon of freedom; 'till the distant sound

Of tolling Curfew warns me to depart.

Thus under tyrant power I groan, oppress'd

With worse than slavery; yet my free-born soul

Her native warmth forgets not, nor will brook

Menace or taunt from proud insulting peer:

But summons to the field the doughty foe

In single combat, 'midst th' impartial throng,

There to decide our fate. Oft too enflam'd

With mutual rage, two rival armies meet

Of youthful warriors; kindling at the fight,

My soul is fill'd with vast heroic thoughts,

Trusting, in martial glory, to surpass

Roman or Grecian chief; instant, with shouts

The mingling squadrons join the horrid fray;

No need of cannon, or the murd'rous steel,

Wide-wasting; nature, rage our arms supplies.

Fragments of rocks are hurl'd, and showers of stones

3   Obscure

Obscure the day; nor less the brawny arm,
Or knotted club avail : high in the midst
Are seen the mighty Chiefs, thro' hosts of foes
Mowing their way; and now, with tenfold rage,
The combat burns, full many a sanguine stream
Distains the field, and many a veteran brave
Lies prostrate; loud triumphant shouts ascend
By turns from either host; each claims the palm
Of glorious conquest; nor till night's dun shades
Involve the sky, the doubtful conflict ends.

Thus when rebellion shook the thrones of heav'n,
And all th' eternal powers in battle met,
High o'er the rest, with vast gigantic strides,
The godlike leaders, on th' embattled plain,
Came tow'ring, breathing forth revenge and fate;
Nor less terrific join'd the inferior hosts
Of angel warriors, when encount'ring hills,
Tore the rent concave,—flashing with the blaze
Of fiery arms, and lightnings, not of Jove;
All heav'n resounded, and th' astonish'd deeps
Of chaos bellow'd with the monstrous roar.

THE

THE OXONIAN.

PARENT of light and fong, whatever name,
Phœbus, or Mithras, more delight thine ear;
The Mufe, with rapture, hails thy rifing beams,
Burft from her drear confinement, where the hand
Of vaunting tyranny repreft her rage,
And damp'd her flagging wing, now borne aloft
To milder regions, and more genial foils.

No more the Pædagogue, with brandifh'd rod,
Annoys my fides, nor ftuns with deathful founds
My ftartled ears; for now, with tranfport heard,
The joyful mandate fummons me away,
To where fam'd Ifis rolls her laureate wave;
On whofe gay banks an ancient city ftands,
Crown'd with an hundred fpires, and fwelling domes
Modern, or Gothic, ftately to the view:
Hither, 'tis faid, from Athens' widow'd bow'rs
By Perfian pride and civil rage expell'd,
Dame Wifdom fled of yore, and with her came,

I   Leaving

Leaving the fabled haunts of Caftaly,

Nine beauteous maids, who boaft their birth from Jove:

High on their pinnacles enthron'd they reign,

  * " To us invifible, or dimly feen,"

Except by foaring fancy's keener glance.

Around their fhrines, from Britain's fartheft bound,

Array'd in fables, croud a motley race;

Diftinct with various titles, and degrees

As various—high above the reft appear

Two forms of more majeftic port and mien,

Whofe foverain rule the toga'd race obey,

Hight *Proctors*; by their fleeves of ominous fweep,

Of Genoa's looms the fam'd produce, well known,

And dreaded; thefe in order next, and next

In dignity, a tribe of fages ftand,

Dreadful with *Tippet*, fource of dire difmay

To Frefhmen, and the whole unbearded race;

Their office to fupport and poife the fcale

Of fteady juftice, from the peaceful fhades

Of fcience to repel the barbarous fons

Of infolence, and faction's wild uproar;

Nor are there wanting, who, with ponderous mace,

---

    * Milton's Paradife Loft.

May

May add to mild reproofs vindictive blows,
Full often rued by many a heedlefs wight.

But now array'd in like myflerious ftole,
With flowing band, that faintly ornament,
Hung waving from my chin, I iffue forth
To feek the manfion of a learned fage,
Y'clep'd a Tutor; him aloof I ken,
On elbows twain of antient chair reclin'd,
With cobwebs hung, by time's fharp tooth defac'd,
Midft volumes pil'd on volumes all around,
And dufty manufcripts; treafures I ween
Of antient lore : He fullen from his chair
Reclines not, 'till with many an aukward bow
And ftrain right humble I implore his grace.
Queftions the fage propofes, dark, perplex'd;
Of various import—and to found my fkill
O'er many an author turns, to me well known,
Virgil or Horace, or the dreadful page
Of Homer, name accurft—defcending hence
His fteps at awful diftance I purfue,
Admiring much my ftrange unwonted garb,
And wond'rous head-piece; till at length we reach
The manfion of a venerable Seer,

Second alone of all the letter'd race,

Who opes a mighty volume, graced with rows

Of various names, in feemly order rang'd;

'Midft thefe the humbleft of the mufe's train

Enrolls his name: and Ifis hails her fon.

Some myftic founds pronounc'd, with trembling lips

The facred page I kifs, and from his hand

A book receive, of fmall regard to fee,

With godly counfels fraught, and wholefome rules;

Which ill betide the wight who dares offend.

The wonted fees difcharg'd, I hafte away

To join the circle of my old compeers,

Sever'd by cruel fate—The hearty fhake,

The friendly welcome, go alternate round:

And that bleft day, 'till eve's remoteft hour,

Is facred to our joys—Its choiceft ftores

The genial larder opes; exhaufted deep,

Even to its inmoft hoards, the buttery groans.

But now the bottle rolls its ample round,

Kindling to rapture each congenial foul;

The Lurft of merriment, the joyous catch

Ring round the roofs inceffant—much is talk'd

Of paft exploits, and grievous tafks impos'd

By former tyrants; tyrants now no more.

Tranfported

Tranfported with the thought, in frantic joy
I raife my arm, and 'midft furrounding fhouts,
Quaff the full bumper; ah *full* dearly rued!
Stern fortune, thus ev'n in the cup of blifs
To mix the dregs of woe—a deadly hue
Sudden invefts my cheeks, my fainting foul
Is fill'd with horrid loathings and ftrange pangs,
Unfelt before, convulfing all my frame:
Med'cines are vain, or ferve but to augment
My grievous plight, 'till fome experienc'd friend
Lead me to neighb'ring couch, where grateful fleep
Soon o'er my fenfes fheds her opiate balm.

Heard with lefs terror, now, the tolling bell
Summons my footfteps to that awful dome,
Whofe gaudy windows, all fuperbly dight
With various tints, and quaint hiftoric lore,
Tempt from devotion's page the roving eye—
Myfterious ftudies next my thoughts employ;
Figures and lines, with nicest art to range,
Oblique or fquare, and time, and mode, and fpace,
Perplex my brains—Now logic, rugged maid,
Opens her ftores profound, the wavering mind
To fix aright, and guide the excentric thought:

Such

Sage doctrines, nathlefs unreftrain'd I rove
At large, and riot in fucceflive rounds
Of new delight : Now up the filver ftream
To Medley's bowers, or Godftowe's fam'd retreat,
Straining each nerve, I urge the dancing fkiff;
Or, rufhing headlong down the perilous fteep,
Rouze the fly Reynard from his dark abode :
Or, if inclement vapours load the fky,
Tennis awhile the heavy hours beguiles ;
Or, at the billiards fatal board, I ftake
With anxious heart, the laft fad remnant coin.

Tutors may chide, and angry fires withhold
The wonted largefs, their united rage
I wreck not; * Ticking, gentleft maid, fupports
My finking fame, and all my woes beguiles.
O fairer far than all that Greece, or Rome,
In vaunting ftrain, of nymph or goddefs tell ;
To thee a thoufand temples pierce the fkies :
To thee a thoufand altars ever fmoke :
Great queen of *Arts*, without whofe chearing ray,

* Hail, Ticking ! guardian of diftrefs—
PANEGYRIC ON OXFORD ALE.

Science

Science would droop, and genius muſt expire.

Raiſing one general pray'r, of every rank

Unnumber'd ſuppliants throng thy crouded courts.

To thee, the haughty doctor, rais'd on high

To learning's loftieſt ſeats, tho' far renown'd,

Cringes ſubmiſſive; thee with all his arts

The ſubtle lawyer ſeeks, nor heeds the voice

Of bailiff thundering at his neighbour's gates.

Propitious power, my lyre ſhall ſtill be ſtrung

To ſing thy praiſe, my pencil ſtill prepar'd

To paint thy charms—and well they may, I ween,

For thine the pencil is, and thine the lyre!

Whether the grape's rich juice regales my ſoul,

Or from the potent bowl I quaff new life,

Abhorrent ſtill, I loath the nauſeous fumes

Of that deteſted weed, *Virginia* hight,

Which the ſage Don, in ſpiral clouds exhales,

Frequent and full, as o'er his drowſy malt

Gravely he nods—Be mine that milder leaf

Which Rowley's patriot hand, with ſtudious care,

From hill, or wood, or flowery vale ſelects :

Cheer'd with its genial vapours oft I lounge

Beneath

Beneath the matron's * roofs, or thine, O Kemp,

Mistaken patriot, as, in high debate,

Of British freedom, and of British herb,

We reason much, nor weightier thoughts employ

My tranquil mind, but how the mantling bowl

With sweet, with sour, with spirit rightly mix'd,

May be replenish'd; oft by these inspir'd

From street to street, beneath the moon's pale beam,

Heedless I stray, if haply *Proctor's* voice

Check not my progress—*Siste*—deathful sound,

" What † should I do, or whither turn—amaz'd,

Confounded," down some narrow lane I scower

Of fam'd St. Thomas, virtue's chaste retreat:

But vain my flight, for ruffian's cruel palms

Arrest my steps, and to the offended power

Force me reluctant——he aloud exclaims

Of broken faith, and violated laws,

Full many a tale he adds, of deep import,

And then with mandate stern, to college dooms

Me, hapless wight, with dreadful fines amers'd,

" * Matron of Matrons, Martha Baggs."

Oxford Sausage.

† The Splendid Shilling.

I   Till

Till one long moon revolves her tedious round :

Some godly author, Tillotſon perchance,

Or moral bard to conn, .with heart full ſad.

There long I ſigh unfriended, and alone,

Unleſs ſome dun aſcend my lofty dome,

At firſt with gentle foot, and ſuppliant voice,

But oft denied, and bolder grown, he adds

Vindictive menace, and before my eyes

Diſplays the horrors of that antient fort *,

Drear manſion, where the ſullen debtor pines,

'Midſt circling gloom, and hunger's cruel rage :

While reſtleſs fancy to my ſight preſents

That dreaded volume †, whoſe recording page

Brands, with eternal infamy, the wretch,.

Incorrigible deem'd, whom dire miſdeeds

Of darker ſtain diſgrace : me Phœbus flies,

And all the tuneful nine, tho' oft I try

With feeble nerve to ſtring my uſeleſs lyre—

---

* The caſtle of Oxford, erected by Robert D'Oilie, A. D. 1071, now converted into the county gaol:——The ſtory is well known of a deſcendant of this founder, who being aſked how he came into that place, replied, " by right of inheritance."

† Vulgo dictum, the Black Book, in which, if any member of the univerſity has the misfortune to have his name enrolled, he is totally excluded from attaining any privilege, or taking his degree.

K

The

The time elaps'd, with throbbing heart I feek
The dreaded feer, and to his hand prefent
The letter'd page; with brow auftere he reads
And bids me, from experience wife, beware
To roufe, a fecond time, his fleeping ire——

    Thrice happy fons of *Cam*, whom *Proctor's* rage
Rarely molefts, whether your fnorting fteeds
Snuff from afar Newmarket's well known breeze;
Or furious pant to gain the verdant heights
Of * Gog-magog——O fkill'd with dexterous hand
To fmack the thong, and guide the aerial car;
By * Trumpington's or * Barnwell's blooming dames,
Kenn'd with amaze: How does each Ifis beau
Envy your lot!——Slaves to no fervile laws,
That pinion down their fancy, you difport
In gaudy filks, and various tinctur'd vefts,
Beft fnares for female hearts; our humbler garbs
Subfufc, or fable, fcarcely tempt the glance
Of wifhful nymph, tho' many a nymph we boaft,
As blithe, as blooming, and as bright as your's——

    Why fhould the mufe of direr evils fing,
When *Ruftication*, in her harpy fangs,

* Places well known at Cambridge.

Hurries.

Hurries the wretch, from joy and Isis far,

In sylvan solitudes to waste his youth,

'Midst chiding aunts, and antiquated maids ?

Or why, that last sad fate the wretched prove,

Exil'd for ever from her sacred haunts,

To roam, like Adam, thro' the desart earth,

" * With all the world before them, where to choose

" Their place of rest," yet after all find none.

Spurning each youthful folly, wiser I

Ascend, with graduate splendor, to the heights

Of classic dignity ; in time perchance

May wield the fasces of *proctorial* power,

And be myself that Don, so lately fear'd.

---

* Milton's Paradise Lost.

NETHERBY.

PREFACE.

*N*Etherby is fituated on the borders of Cumberland, twelve miles north of Carlifle; and was formerly a Roman ftation: the *Caftro Exploratorum* of Antoninus. From the many valuable remains of antiquity, continually found on, or near, this fpot, it is conjectured that the famous Æfica ftood not far diftant; efpecially as the river Efk, from which its name is derived, runs through thefe grounds. The perpetual feuds that fubfifted on the borders, between the Englifh and Scots, before the Union of the two nations, with the particular circumftance of the *debateable land*, which, at prefent, makes a part of the eftate; the eruption of *Solway Mofs* which happened in 1771; added to the prefent improved and beautiful ftate of *Netherby*, afforded ample room for luxuriant defcription, and the wantonnefs of a poetical imagination.

" *Netherby*——The feat of the Rev. Dr. Graham, placed on a
" rifing ground, wafhed by the Efk, and commanding an extenfive
" view; more pleafing to Dr. Graham, as he fees from it a creation
" of his own; lands that eighteen years ago were in a ftate of na-
" ture, the people idle and bad, ftill retaining a fmack of the feudal
" manners: fcarce a hedge to be feen: and a total ignorance prevailed
" of even coal and lime. His improving fpirit foon wrought a great
" change in thefe parts: his example inftilled into the inhabitants an
" inclination

3

" inclination to induſtry : and they ſoon found the difference between
" ſloth and its concomitants, dirt and beggary, and the plenty that a
" right application of the arts of huſbandry brought among them.
" They lay in the midſt of a rich country, yet ſtarved in it : but in
" a ſmall ſpace they found that inſtead of a produce that hardly ſup-
" ported themſelves, they were enabled to raiſe even ſupplies for their
" neighbours : that much of their land was ſo kindly as to bear corn
" for many years ſucceſſively, without help of manure, and for the
" more ungrateful ſoils, that there were limeſtones to be had and
" coal to burn them.——The wild tract ſoon appeared in form of
" verdant meadows and fruitful corn-fields : from the firſt, they were
" ſoon able to ſend to diſtant places, cattle and butter : and their
" arable lands enabled them to maintain a commerce as far as Lan-
" caſhire in corn.

" By ſignifies a habitation ; thus, there are three camps or ſtations,
" with this termination, not very remote from one another; Netherby,
" Middleby, and Overby." Mr. Pennant's Tour in Scotland.
Vol. II. p. 64.

ARGUMENT.

A comparative view of the prefent flourishing ftate of Netherby, *with its former defolate appearance. Addrefs to Induftry. Conqueft of Britain by Cæfar. The firft irruption of the Scots—Their repulfe by the Roman legions, under Julius Agricola. The wall of Severus. Æfica. Britain fucceffively conquered by the Saxons, the Danes, the Normans. Feudal Syftem. Magna Charta. General view of the borders, before the Union—After the Union. The particular improvements at Netherby. Eruption of Solway Mofs. Defcription of the grounds about Netherby. Skiddaw. Ellen Irvine. The houfe defcribed. Concluding with a view of the new church building on the eftate.*

L

N E-

N E T H E R B Y.

A R E thefe the regions, where, from age to age,
Contending nations ftrove, with mutual rage;
Her barren wing, where brooding famine fpread;
And frantic faction rear'd her ghaftly head?
How chang'd the fcene—what glorious profpects rife;
Where-e'er around I turn my wond'ring eyes!
Here guardian peace, here fmiling culture reigns,
And endlefs plenty cloaths the fertile plains.
Yon ftream * that, erft, impurpled with the flain,
In many a fanguine billow fought the main,
Now guiltlefs rolls, and views, with confcious pride,
Luxuriant landfcapes glitter on her fide;
A thoufand hills with wealth and verdure crown'd,
And vales in rich profufion fmiling round.
No more they ring with battles fierce alarms,
No trumpets early clangors rouze to arms;

* The Elk.

L 2

Echoes

Echoes of rapture, now, alone, they hear,
The ploughman's whiftle, or the fportfman's cheer—
What tho' bleak Boreas oft deform the day,
Or frequent ftorms obfcure the genial ray,
Th' induftrious fwain, with firm, undaunted foul,
Contemns his rage, and bids the tempeft roll:
Mark, how fereue, his honeft front defies
The wildeft fury of the beating fkies:
Still as the fhining fhare the furrow turns,
His bofom with rekindled ardour burns;
By long experience taught, the grateful foil,
With intereft, will repay his ufeful toil.

Hail Induftry, rough virtue's hardy child;
Whofe fmiling prefence chears the lonely wild:
At thy kind touch the rock, relenting, blooms,
And Eden fprings, 'midft Lapland's frozen glooms.
The rapid river, rolling in its courfe,
Thy hand arrefts, and curbs its headlong force;
The fwelling deep's tumultuous fury bounds,
And chains its waves with everlafting mounds.
Empires and ftates to thee their greatnefs owe,
From thee their wealth, their power, their fplendor flow;

Rifing

Rifing in glory, as they court thy fway,
By thee they flourifh, and with thee decay.

Long had the mighty Roman Victor hurl'd
Slaughter and rapine o'er the wafted world :
Unconquer'd yet, remote, Britannia ftood
Safe 'midft her native cliffs, and guardian flood.
He mark'd the dangers of her ftormy fhore,
He heard the breaking waves eternal roar;
But, flufh'd with conqueft, his undaunted mind
Brav'd all the rage of feas and ftorms combin'd.
In vain, the favages his arms oppofe,
His legions burft their way thro' hofts of foes;
Her rocks they fcale, her tracklefs defarts pierce,
They tame her monfters, and her fons, more fierce.
Swift o'er the land the Roman arts increafe,
And culture triumphs, with returning peace :
With fudden verdure, lo! the valleys fmile,
And rifing plenty crowns the blooming ifle.

Far to the North, beyond where Tweed's fair pride,
Thro' velvet meadows rolls her amber tide;
Or Cumbria's lofty mountains, rifing round,
Of ancient Britain, form'd th' extended bound :

There

There dwelt a race, inur'd to want and toil,
The sons of Caledonia's defart foil;
Thefe view'd the neighb'ring ftate, with jealous eyes,
And rufh'd, exulting, on the beauteous prize.
They pour'd their armies o'er the fertile plain,
Tore ev'ry fence, and reap'd the untimely grain :
The Britons fhrink, unequal, from the fight,
And bend, to diftant fields, their hafty flight.
Nought can withftand the fell barbarian's rage,
Nor tears nor fhrieks their favage fouls affuage,
Nor fex, nor age, their murd'rous weapons fpare,
Nor from the temples holy fhrines forbear ;
With impious hand, they quench the hallow'd fire ;
While the fage Druids, 'midft their rites, expire.

To quell their pride, th' imperial bards advance,
Their myriads crouch beneath the Roman lance ;
Aloft the victor-hofts * their flag difplay,
The Britifh youth, with joy, the fign obey ;
On the proud foe the vengeful blow returns,
While every breaft with great refentment burns : .

* The General who finally eftablifhed the dominion of the Romans in this ifland was Julius Agricola ; who governed it in the reigns of Vefpafian, Titus, and Domitian. He carried his victorious arms to the moft northern extremity of it, and pierced into the remote forefts and mountains of Caledonia, which were before deemed inacceffible.

Onward

Onward they ruſh, like ſome reſiſtleſs flood,

And deluge all his waſted realms with blood—

His rocks, his mountains, every deſart heath,

Reſponſive echo to the ſhrieks of death !

Thus, full aveng'd, the ſwains, with anxious care,

The trampled fence and mural breach repair ;

Their friendly aid the generous Romans lend ;

Their new allies from rapine to defend :

And lo, a mighty rampart * rears its head ;

While nations triumph in its guardian ſhade ;

Winding o'er hill and vale, from Solway's ſhores,

To where the Tyne his diſtant current pours :

The lofty tow'rs with ſhining warriors blaze,

Whoſe helmets glitter with the morning rays :

Dauntleſs they ſtand, and ſtretch the ſounding bow,

And dart ſwift vengeance on the diſtant foe.

Then flouriſh'd thy fair pride, illuſtrious town † ;

Tho fate hath daſh'd thy gilded temples down !|

What tho' thy beauteous turrets beam'd on high,

And thy ſtrong bulwarks tower'd amidſt the ſky ;

Not all thy ſtrength, nor beauty, could withſtand

Faction's fell rage, nor ſtop the plunderer's hand.

* The wall of Severus, extending from Bullneſs on the Solway Firth quite acroſs the kingdom to Newcaſtle.

† Æſica. See Camden's Britannia.

The feat of heroes, gen'rous, rough and bold,
Oft thro' thy gates the tide of battle roll'd—
Methinks I hear the rattling chariot bound,
And the bold fteed impatient paw the ground;
Monarchs and chiefs, the glory of mankind,
Beneath thy domes, their laurel'd heads reclin'd;
Like them, fhall flourifh thy immortal name,
Partake their honours, and enjoy their fame.
The lab'ring hind, as o'er thefe hallow'd plains,
(Where reft intomb'd thy grandeur's proud remains,)
He guides the fhare, beholds, with wild furprize,
Helmets and fpears, of wond'rous make and fize;
* Urns, altars, ftatues, which ftrange fculptures grace,
And fondly ftrives the myftic lore to trace;
From mould'ring coins the facred ruft he clears,
And mars the labour of a thoufand years.
Pleas'd fome great prince or hero to behold,
But more delighted with the glift'ning gold.

Queen of the world, at length, majeftic Rome
Beheld, and trembled at her haft'ning doom;
Opprefs'd with grandeur's vaft incumbent weight,
The fenate fcarce upheld the finking ftate;

---

* The reader will find, in Mr. Pennant, a particular account of all the curiofities at Netherby, with engravings of the principal.

Her

Her pamper'd fons, unlike their valiant fires,

Retain no patriot rage, no martial fires;

On beds of filk they wafte the tedious day,

Or feebly trill the foft, unmanly lay.

Unable to repel the barbarous hofts,

That pour'd their fury on her plunder'd coafts,

She calls her braveft fons from ev'ry fhore,

In black'ning fwarms the diftant legions pour,

From burning realms, where fouthern deeps refound,

From Britain's coafts, from Afia's fartheft bound :

While vengeance o'er the imperial city lours,

And frantic difcord fhakes her hundred towers.

The drooping Britons, feiz'd with equal dread,

Beheld their brave allies and conquerors fled,

The guardians of their ftate; nor vain their fears,

High on the wall the infulting Scot appears :

Furious from native courage, and defpair,

The fiercenefs of his rage, awhile they dare ;

But broke and routed by fuperior force,

To diftant plains, once more, they bend their courfe :

The fhouting foe purfues, with barbarous rage,

And the fierce hofts eternal conflict wage ;

Till Britain's loftieft hills, alone, afford,

Her offspring refuge from the murd'rous fword.

M   But

But now, imperial Rome in aſhes laid,
Her laurels blaſted, and her ſtrength decay'd;
Germania's veteran bands, in war renown'd,
With terror aw'd the wond'ring nations round:
Hengiſt and Horſa, chiefs of mightier name,
Shone foremoſt on the bright record of fame;
Like gods, they tower'd amidſt the ſons of earth,
As from thoſe powers * they trac'd their vaunted birth.
To theſe brave chiefs the Britons turn their eyes,
On them alone their laſt fond hope relies:
The hero comes; but not, with vengeful hand,
From rapine's graſp to wreſt the bleeding land;
With their triumphant foes their faithleſs train,
In barbarous league, they join, and rivet every chain.

In vain the Druid ſmites the magic ſtring,
In vain the rocks with choral warblings ring;
Tho' oft Britannia rais'd her feeble ſhield,
Tho' oft their braveſt veterans ſtrew'd the field;
Tho' Horſa's ſelf, deſcended from the ſkies,
Pour'd forth his life, a glorious ſacrifice,

* They were reputed to be deſcended from their god Woden.

Beneath

Beneath a Briton's fpear—yet ftill, in vain,
She ftrove her ravifh'd honours to regain;
Refiftlefs Hengift thunder'd round the land,
And tore the fceptre from her trembling hand;
At length fhe funk beneath the galling yoke,
Her rage extinct, her martial fpirit broke;
Pale, at his feet, her proftrate genius lay,
While flaughter mark'd the victor's crimfon way.

The Saxon triumph'd, till the fiercer Dane,
In pomp, advancing o'er the whitening main,
Rear'd his infulting Raven * on her fhore,
And fwell'd her rivers with unufual gore;
Where-e'er he treads, the furies howl around,
While his fell footfteps blaft the with'ring ground:
Both yield, at length, to William's conquering fword,
And harrafs'd Britain own'd a *Norman* lord.
Why fhould the mufe of feudal power relate,
The haughty lord's, or humbler vaffal's fate;

---

* The famous Reafen, or enchanted ftandard, is here alluded to, in which the Danes put
great confidence. It contained the figure of a raven, which had been inwove by the three
fifteis of Hingua and Hubba with many magical incantations, the flappings of whofe wings
was regarded as the certain prefage of victory.

Hovr

How petty Kings each others realms invade,

By turns, are murder'd, conquer'd, or betray'd?

Their fame, their fortunes, she difdains to fing;

Oblivion fhade them with thy dufky wing.

With joy fhe haftens to that happier age,

In which, fuperior to oppreffion's rage,

The firm, undaunted barons, dar'd withftand

A tyrant's frown, and check'd his guilty hand :

When Juftice darted from the radiant fky,

When vengeance wav'd her flaming fword on high;

When rifing freedom dawn'd upon our ifle,

And chear'd the nation with her rofeate fmile :

When laws, which time nor tyrants fhall efface,

Founded on wifdom's and on virtue's bafe,

Of this wide empire form'd the mighty bound;

The pride, the wonder of the nations round !

Then culture rais'd once more her drooping head,

And arts, that lay in long oblivion dead,

Sprang to new life—then commerce gave her fail,

With fwelling pomp to flutter in the gale;

Our navies fail'd to many a diftant fhore,

That now firft heard the Britifh lion roar—

The peaceful fwain fecurely turn'd the foil,

And reap'd, fecure, the produce of his toil :

In

In one firm league the various nations join,

Loft, undiftinguifh'd, in the Englifh line;

All but the haughty Scot—whofe ftubborn foul *

Nor Henry's † conquering fquadrons could controul,

Nor fiercer Edward‡; tho' fuch heaps of flain,

Expiring, groan'd on Falkirk's fatal plain;

And blafted by malignant fortune's frown,

The captive Baliol wail'd his plunder'd crown.

Wide o'er the borders rang'd a favage band,

That fcatter'd flames and ravage round the land:

Where-e'er fair culture's beauteous hand was feen,

Their favage footfteps crufh'd the rifing green;

And ev'ry flower that bloffom'd on the mead,

Shrunk from their rage, and droop'd its wither'd head.

What gloomy profpects open on my eyes!

On every fide, what fcenes of horror rife!

* The Author is very far from meaning by this, or any other expreffion that may occur in this Poem, to revive any idea of former animofities between two nations at prefent fo happily united under one head. What he has written, is in conformity to the truth of hiftory, and is by no means intended as a reflection on a people who are diftinguifhed by their liberal hofpitality to ftrangers, as the Author has experienced; who is happy in this opportunity of expreffing his grateful acknowledgments.

† Henry I.

‡ Edward I. who, at the battle of Falkirk, entirely routed and put to flight the whole Scottifh army. Some hiftorians make the lofs of the Scots amount to fifty or fixty thoufand men; certain it is they never fuffered a greater lofs, or one that feemed to threaten more inevitable ruin to their country.

I fee

I fee each beauteous vale with weeds o'erfpread;
The fields neglected, and their owners fled;
Scarce can the pining natives, that remain,
By wretched arts their wretched lives fuftain:
Nor branching tree, nor verdant hedge appears,
Nor voice, nor found, the lonely defart chears;
Save where the bittern fcreams, with clam'rous throat,
Refponfive to the raven's hoarfer note,
That flaps her wing 'gainft yonder mould'ring tower;
The fole furviving pledge of Roman power.

The glorious period *, wifh'd fo long in vain,
Breaks forth at length in Anna's golden reign;
When the fame laws each happy nation bind,
In ftricteft league by her wife councils join'd:
When either triumphs in Britannia's name,
Their pow'r, their int'reft, and their King, the fame.
And fee, from far, yon glitt'ring ftar † appear,
Whofe luftre gilds our weftern hemifphere;
Thefe plains, opprefs'd with one long wintry night,
Feel the warm influence of its genial light:

* The Union.

† The happinefs and fecurity derived from the glorious Revolution are here alluded to,
and the general encouragement given to agriculture by late parliaments.——Mr. Gray fays,
    " The ftar of Brunfwick fhines ferene."

Green

Green rifing woods the lofty hills adorn,
The fruitful valleys fmile with waving corn;
But ftretch'd immenfe, beneath more northern fkies,
Uncultur'd ftill the barren region lies—

    Graham beheld, and, in his prudent mind,
Pond'ring awhile, the beauteous plan defign'd:
He mark'd the hallow'd fcene, where, many an age,
Beheld of old the Britifh hofts engage;
He faw the fwain, with toil and want opprefs'd,
He faw—and manly pity heav'd his breaft.
He taught the wild, unfkilful hind, to rear
The tender plant, and mark the varying year;
When the moift earth, enrich'd with genial rain,
Expects, impatient, the protracted grain;
When fpreading fhoots the pruning hand implore,
Or autumn waves, mature, his yellow ftore.
And lo! a race, in native wildnefs rude,
That long had rang'd the dreary folitude,
The meagre fons of floth and pale difeafe,
Spring from their trance—their rufty fhares they feize;
They raife the fence, they lift the pond'rous load,
And form the ditch, and mark the future road.
Their hard'ning limbs the tempeft's rage fuftain,
While manlier vigour flows in ev'ry vein;

3

Heav'ns!

Heav'ns! with what rival zeal they toil, they fweat,
Beneath th' inclement blaft, or fcorching heat,
Their lord, with glorious hopes, their labours chears,
And paints the plenty of approaching years;
He marks the boundaries of ev'ry field,
Nor fcorns himfelf the weighty prong to wield,
To break the clod, to crufh the noxious weed,
Or fcatter, as he treads, the lib'ral feed.

The defart foon in lovelier garb appears,
And ev'ry field the fmile of plenty wears:
Increafing years increafing treafures bring,
With livelier verdure blooms returning fpring;
The fwains, tranfported, view the grateful foil,
And triumph in the meed of many a toil.
When lo! a fcene more dark and dreadful rofe,
Than e'er had fwell'd the lift of former woes;
A tyrant, fiercer than the Danifh band,
Spread defolation o'er the fmiling land.
Near that fam'd fpot where, * ftung with fhame and grief,
Scotia's bold warriors fpurn'd a minion chief:

---

* James V. having appointed his favourite, Oliver Sinclair, to command the army acting againft Henry King of England, the Scots refented the indignity, refufed to ferve under him, and to a man laid down their arms.

And,

And, tho' more fkill'd to conquer than to yield,
Bade Henry triumph on a bloodlefs field.
Full many a league a mighty fwamp extends;
The dufky heath by gentle flope afcends:
The rafh, advent'rous ftep will foon betray,
And whelm the wight, incautious of his way.
Woe to the trav'ler, whofe benighted feet,
By chance, fhall ftumble on this lone retreat;
Soon fhall the hopelefs wand'rer meet his doom,
Bewilder'd 'midft the vaft incumbent gloom:
Some faithlefs bog fhall quickly clofe him round,
Some chafm fhall fwallow in its gulph profound.
This vaft morafs—oh grant, ye powers above,
Thefe fields may never more its fury prove——
Diffolv'd by floods, and fwol'n with mighty rains,
Pour'd its black deluge o'er the neighbouring plains.
Mark how the gloomy ocean, gath'ring round,
Indignant fwells, and burfts th' oppofing mound:
Ah fee—thro' yonder beauteous vale * it fpreads,
Whelming, at once, an hundred fertile meads;

Then,

---

* " A tract, diftinguifhed for its fertility and beauty, ran in form of a valley for fome fpace in view of Netherby; it had been finely reclaimed from its original ftate, prettily divided, well planted with hedges, and well peopled: the ground, originally not worth fixpence an acre, was improved to the value of thirty fhillings. I faw it in that fituation in the year

1769:

Then, bearing onward, with refiftlefs force,

Sweeps herds and houfes in its dreadful courfe;

Till Efk's fair tide its mingling billows ftain,

That roll with added fury to the main.

The trembling fwains, with terror and amaze,.

Diftracted on the cruel fpoiler gaze—

Such frantic horror glar'd in ev'ry face,

As feiz'd of old the wild, aftonifh'd race,

That faw Vefuvius firft in thunder pour.

Fragments of rocks, and ftreams of molten ore;.

Whofe fiery volumes,blaft their green alcoves,

Their loaded vineyards, and.their bending groves——.

1769: at this time a melancholy extent of black turbery,.the eruption of Solway-Mofs,
having in a few days covered grafs and corn, levelled the boundaries of almoft every farm,
deftroyed moft of the houfes, and drove the poor inhabitants to the utmoft diftrefs; till they
found (which was not long) from their landlord every relief that.a humane mind could fug-
geft. Solway-Mofs confifts of fixteen hundred acres; lies fome height above the cultivated
tract, and feems to have been nothing but a collection of thin peaty mud: the furface itfelf
was always fo near the ftate of·a quagmire that in moft places it was unfafe for any thing
heavier than a fportfman to venture on, even in the drieft fummer.. The fhell or cruft that
kept this liquid within bounds, neareft to the valley, was at firft of fufficient ftrength to contain it, but by the imprudence of the peat-diggers, who were·continually working on that
fide, became at length fo weakened, as not to be able any longer to refift the weight preffing
on it: the fluidity of the Mofs was likewife greatly increafed by three days rain of unufual
violence, which preceded the eruption. About three hundred acres of mofs,were thus dif-
charged, and about four hundred of land covered; but providentially not a human life loft."
Mr. Pennant's Tour, p. 64, where may be found a more particular account of this event.

Untaught

Untaught fuch dire extremes of fate to bear,
The fullen ruftic dropp'd, in wan defpair:
Extended on the damp, unwholefome earth,
He curft the baleful moment of his birth;
The tear of anguifh trembles in his eye,
And his ftrong bofom heaves the frequent figh.
With wilder grief the frantic females rave,
And bound, with horror, from the monfter wave;
While from their breafts their trembling infants hung,
And, confcious of their fate, more clofely clung.

But foon their lord, opprefs'd with generous grief,
To each defponding wretch affords relief;
His lib'ral hand diffufive plenty pours:
Benevolence unlocks her genial ftores:
He hears their plaints; he calms the burfting figh,
And wipes the falling tear from ev'ry eye.
The fwains, with chearfulnefs, renew their toil,
And lighten, of its load, the burthen'd foil;
The fields * once more their verdant hue refume,
And with fuperior pride and beauty bloom.

---

* Since Mr. Pennant vifited this place, fome part of the Mofs has, with infinite labour and expence, been removed; a great part however ftill remains covered: but this tract is not of fuch extent, as to interrupt the pleafure that arifes from a general view of the country.

How

How wide thefe furs their infant branches fpread,
And wave their wanton foliage o'er my head!
Already, from the fultry dog's ftar heat,
Their friendly fhades afford a kind retreat;
Ambitious to repay his guardian care,
Who bade their tow'ring fummits rife in air.——
Let others boaft the proud, afpiring pile,
Columns and fanes, in ev'ry various ftyle;
With fwelling arches bound the folemn glade,
Or thunder down the fteep the loud cafcade;
While thro' the fhades, as fearful of the light,
The polifh'd ftatue glances on the fight,
Here, Venus fmiles, 'midft circling boughs conceal'd,
And there, Minerva feems to fhake her fhield.
Nature, great architect, thefe plains arrays,
In pomp, beyond what mimic art difplays;
To them no works of foreign pride are known,
Nor other bound, but heavn'n's wide arch alone——
Majeftic thro' the midft, with murm'ring roar,
See winding Efk his rapid current pour;
On the bright wave the fportive falmon play,
And bound and gliften in the noon-tide ray.

There

There tow'ring Skiddaw *, wrapt in awful fhade,
Monarch of mountains, rears his mighty head,
Dark'ning with frowns fair Kefwick's beauteous vale,
He views beneath the gath'ring tempefts fail,.
Secure, nor heeds the rolling thunder's rage;
Tho' Scruffel † trembling marks the dire prefage.

Pierc'd with congenial grief, my fancy flies
To where Kirkonnel's neighb'ring woods arife;
There, bending o'er the beauteous Ellen's ‡ tomb,
She weeps the wretched nymph's untimely doom.
So fair a plant, old Kirtle's wand'ring tide
Had never cherifh'd on its verdant fide;
But oh! what pen her various charms fhall paint,
Here even a Raphael's glowing tints were faint :
Thofe radiant eyes, where lambent lightnings play,
Thofe coral lips, that breathe the fweets of May;

* Skiddaw is plainly feen at the diftance of thirty miles from this feat.
† Alluding to thefe proverbial lines—
> When Skiddaw wears a cap,
> Scruffel wots full well of that.

Scruffel is a mountain in Annandale in Scotland, the inhabitants of which prognofticate good or bad weather, from the mifts that fall or rife on the brow of Skiddaw.
‡ See Mr. Pennant, page 88.

Thofe

Thofe cheeks, that fhame the morning's purple glow,
That bofom, whiter than the pureft fnow :
Around her fport a thoufand laughing loves;
Each breaft is kindled as the virgin moves :
With her foft name, the woods, the valleys rung,
And Ellen's praifes dwelt on ev'ry tongue——
Two rival fwains, of nobler birth and fame,
Together languifh'd in the tender flame ;
Bold Fleming knew to guide the whirling car,
To dart the fpear and ftemm the rage of war ;
In Ardolph's breaft ignobler tranfports roll'd,
He boafts his large domains, his hoards of gold;
With thefe he fought the blooming maid to gain,
Who fpurn'd his proffer'd rreafure with difdain.
The warrior triumph'd in her partial care,
For valour ever wins the gen'rous fair.
With him fhe fparkled in the feftive round,
He fpake, and rapture dwelt in ev'ry found ;
Together, thro' the winding vale they rove,
Together, wander in the lonely grove,
The feather'd warblers catch their tender ftrains,
And wilder mufic floats along the plains.
In rapture, thus, their moments roll'd away,
While fcarce the lover brooks the long delay ;

'Till

'Till Hymen fmil'd propitious from above,
And fhower'd down rofes on the couch of love.

    Ardolph, mean-time, with jealous cares opprefs'd,
Felt ev'ry various paffion tear his breaft;
Rage, hatred, grief in mingling tempefts rife,
Lour on his front, and fire his redd'ning eyes;
All frantic, wild, he fought a darkfome glade,
And proftrate roll'd, beneath th' incumbent fhade;
Then ftarts aghaft, and pours thefe dreadful moans,
While each majeftic oak in concert groans—

" Ye arching glooms, that o'er this wretched head,
" In fable pomp, your friendly horrors fpread;
" And wave, obedient to the fullen gale,
" That murmurs, hoarfe, along the lonely vale:
" Thou moon, that glancing on yon diftant ftream,
" Dart'ft thro' the quiv'ring fhades a filver gleam,
" By you I fwear; hear all ye fylvan powers,
" That haunt this tide and range thefe hallow'd bowers,
" And ftamp my vows: ere day's bright orb arife,
" To deck with kindling light the blufhing fkies;
" The hated wretch this flighted arm fhall feel,
" And pour his life beneath my reeking fteel;
" Yes, when tranfported with thofe blooming charms,
" He finks, all melting, in her circling arms;

Then

" Then fhall my vengeance wake, and fate fhall clafp

" The expiring hero in her chilling grafp—

" Thou too, whom neither vows nor fighs could move,

" Thou fhalt the fiercenefs of my paffion prove;

" How will my bofom glow with rapturous heat,

" How ev'ry pulfe with thrilling tranfport beat,

" As o'er that paradife of fweets I rove,

" And fatiate all my rage, and all my love!"

He fpake, and guided by the moon's pale ray,
Burfts thro' the winding gloom his eager way;
Fierce as he moves, his furious fteps refound;
The dark heath fhakes, the foreft trembles round:
As when, o'er fultry Libya's burning plains,
Some tyger ftalks, the terror of the fwains;
If chance a ftrolling kid, or wanton fawn,
Thoughtlefs of danger, gambol o'er the lawn;
His fiery eyes the panting fpoil furvey,
He bounds and fprings, exulting on his prey—
Such favage tranfports flafh from Ardolph's eyes,
As fudden the devoted wretch he 'fpies,
With his fair fpoufe, beneath a neighb'ring grove,
Reclin'd in all the tendernefs of love.
With headlong rage he plunges in the tide,
Whofe waves alone the hoftile youths divide;

3

And, fpringing tow'rds th' oppofing bank, difplay'd.
To Fleming's ftartled view the vengeful blade :
To fcreen her lover from th' impending blow,
The beauteous nymph oppos'd her breaft of fnow;
Her fnow-white breaft the murd'rous weapon tore,
And pierc'd her heart—that gufh'd in floods of gore :
The trembling hufband clafp'd her, fainting, round,
And eager ftrove to ftanch the ftreaming wound;
While, fondly hanging on his beating breaft,
To his pale cheek her paler cheek fhe preft;
Then fixing ftedfaftly her wifhful eyes,
Effay'd to fpeak, but, choak'd with burfting fighs,
She ftrove in vain—thofe eyes in darknefs roll,
And hov'ring feraphs catch her gafping foul.

Fleming, in frantic horror, feiz'd the blade,
And inftant ftruck the bafe affaffin dead—
Then, with a thoufand ftruggling paffions preft,
He rais'd the pointed dagger to his breaft :
Scarce could his grief the defp'rate deed withftand,
But confcious honour check'd his rifing hand;
" Yes, I will dare to live, and feek, in fight,
" A nobler paffage to the fhades of night :

O   " Come,

" Come, glory come, and fpread thy fmiling charms;

" O bear me to the battle's mad alarms;

" Beat ev'ry drum, let ev'ry trumpet found,

" Till anguifh, in the field of death, be drown'd."

He faid, and rufhing to th' embattled plain,

'Gainft the proud Turk * he led a valiant train;

There glory own'd her fon, and round his head,

Her radiant hands unfading laurels fpread.

But while her choiceft gifts the hero crown'd,

The lover languifh'd with his fecret wound:

Eager he haften'd to his native fhore,

And zephyr's gentleft breezes waft him o'er;

He fought the grove, where lay his lovely bride,

Stretch'd his fond limbs along the turf—and died.

On yonder mount where once, with hoftile pride,

The Roman wav'd his crimfon banner wide;

A graceful ftructure meets the wond'ring fight,

And fills the gazing ftranger with delight:

As o'er thefe vales he rolls his eager eyes,

And fees an † Eden in a defert rife.

---

* He afterwards ferved in the wars againft the Infidels.

† The reader will not think this defcription much exaggerated, who has travelled farther northward than *Netherby*; as the entrance into Scotland, on that fide, for many miles together, bears a moft unpromifing and dreary afpect.

What tho' no ufelefs grandeur deck the dome,
Rich with the fhining fpoils of Greece or Rome;
What tho' no gilded roofs, with high emblaze,
Pour on the dazzled eye their ftreaming rays;
Yet beauty fmiles confefs'd in ev'ry part,
While nature crowns the bold attempts of art :
Here elegance, with ufe, her charms combines,
And thro' the whole with fofter luftre fhines.
No more thefe walls the victor's fhouts prolong,
Echoing the clafh of mail, the martial fong;
Within their bounds refide a gentler train;
Here facred peace and focial virtue reign:
Here, groaning with its freight, the friendly board
Proclaims the bounty of its generous lord;
Here famifh'd travellers forget their woes,
And weary'd ftrangers fink in foft repofe.

To crown the whole, view yon proud fane afcend,
Which, guardian feraphs, with their wings defend !
Behold ! all radiant with celeftial light,
The dome, afcending, fwells upon the fight;
The folemn gates our mufing fouls infpire
With rev'rend awe, and rouze devotion's fire;

O 2

Here oft, as yonder planet lights the day,
Or ev'ning fheds oblique her purple ray,
With conftant zeal fhall bend a youthful train,
And fongs of rapture rend the hallow'd fane.
Hark, what fweet warblings undulate in air,
Glowing with praife, or fraught with fervent pray'r;
While, as they chaunt Jehovah's mighty name,
Thro' ev'ry bofom fpreads the kindred flame;
Their pious vows fhall confecrate the pile,
And heav'n's dread fire receive them with a fmile.

HAGLEY.

HAGLEY.

P R E F A C E.

HAGLEY is fituated in the neighbourhood of Birmingham, on the road leading to Bewdley, in Worcefterfhire, and is not lefs indebted to nature for its beauties than the tafte and genius of the late Lord Lyttelton.

Through a long dark avenue of limes we approach the houfe, which is an elegant modern building, and adorned with paintings of the moft eminent Italian mafters. There are likewife fome bufts and ftatues of great value; thofe of Milton, Shakefpeare, Spenfer, and Dryden, in the library, were made by Scheenmaker, and left by Mr. Pope, at his death, to his lordfhip. The views from the houfe are every way delightful; particularly that on the garden fide. Immediately oppofite, at fome diftance, on the brow of a lawn, ftands a light column, backed by a noble grove; on the left of which the temple of Thefeus prefents itfelf, on the beautiful hill of Witchberry, embofomed in firs; and above this, on a higher eminence, towers the obelifk.

Leaving the houfe we come to the Parifh Church, a fmall Gothic building, in which is a beautiful monument to the memory of Lucy Lyttelton, his lordfhip's firft lady.

Every

Every reader of taste will remember the beautiful monody composed by his lordship on the death of this lady, which does equal honour to the memory of both. On the left of this monument is a small unadorned stone, which acquaints us, that the noble author rests below. This was placed here by his lordship's particular desire, and strongly impresses the mind with an idea of that virtue which sought applause, superior to what man could bestow.

A narrow path leads from hence along the lawn to a gloomy hollow, whose steep banks are covered with large rocky stones, as if rent asunder by some violent concussion of nature. The gushing cascade, on either side, adds to the solemnity of the scene,

We now reascend the bank, and winding to the right, arrive at the Alcove, which is supported by the Palladian bridge, of elegant construction. Never before did the hand of art model, or the eye of fancy behold, a scene so ravishing. The grand cascade tumbling from one rock to another down the embosomed vale; the richness of the woods, and the distant Rotunda that terminates the swelling vista, at once fill the mind with astonishment and pleasure.

Keeping to the left hand of the water, a Portico, on the summit of a rising ground, catches the eye with peculiar grace. We enter, through a small wicket, the environs of the grotto. From a bench under an old oak of surprizing magnitude we have a most pleasing prospect of this retirement; the shrubs and flowers scattered in profusion on the banks, salute us with their fragrance as we penetrate its inmost recesses; where stands a statue of Venus, as just rising from the water: Here are several grotesque stone alcoves, and seats shaded with laurels.

Opposite

trate its inmoft recefies; where ftands a ftatue of Venus, as juft rifing from the water: Here are feveral grotefque ftone alcoves, and feats fhaded with laurels.

Oppofite to thefe is another cafcade, which is decorated with large vitrified cinders, and other ftones of a fhining fubftance, which have a very pleafing effect. This rural folitude is quitted, not without reluctance, and after rifing the fteep afcent, we continue our walk under the fhade of fpacious trees to a bank, on which is an urn, dedicated to the memory of the late Mr. Shenftone.

Turning hence to the left, the rotunda again ftrikes the view, as we walk along the fides of a folitary glen, thick planted with coppice and other trees. Croffing this glen, you arrive at the favourite fpot of the late Mr. Pope, in the midft of a fwelling irregular lawn, entirely furrounded with woods. His lordfhip has erected an urn to the memory of this bard; whom, living, he honoured with his particular friendfhip.

The afcent now becomes bold and fteep, winding amidft a variety of ftately trees, to the higheft eminence in the park; on which is fituated, with great judgment, and not lefs beauty, the Ruin. This venerable pile bears every appearance of antiquity; and we are confirmed in that opinion, by the maffy ftones which have in many places tumbled down from the ruinous walls, and the mouldering towers almoft covered with ivy. But how great is our aftonifhment, when, on a nearer approach, we perceive it to be a ufeful modern ftructure, built for a keeper's lodge, and fo difpofed, as to make it a principal object from feveral feats in the park. Here, indeed, the tafte of the defigner has difplayed itfelf; and his lord-

P

lordfhip,

ship, in leaving one of the towers entire, hath afforded an opportunity of surveying an horizon, which, for its vast extent, and the grandeur and beauty of the objects it displays, is no where to be rivalled.

From hence the path leads to the foot of the Clent Hills, which are situated without the park pale, but amply recompence the labour of ascending them, by the extensive prospect exhibited from their summits. If the stranger chooses to pursue the path on the left, he will find, near the extremity of the park, a handsome Gothic seat, which gives an agreeable view of these hills, the ruin, and the distant country. But pursuing that to the right, through one of the most delicious groves imaginable, he will soon arrive at a seat, which has this inscription:

> Sedes Contemplationis.
> Omnia Vanitas.

Nothing can equal the pleasing serenity we experience in this delightful recess, so admirably adapted to relieve the eye, fatigued with the great and distant objects before presented to its view.

The next object that claims attention is the Hermitage, composed of clumps of wood and roots of old trees, carelessly heaped together. The floor is neatly paved with small pebbles, and is surrounded with a seat, covered with a mat.

We now descend into a vale, where are some pools of water; on every side surrounded by large chesnuts, and spreading elms. Along this vale the path winds through a grove of oaks up a steep hill,

near

near the summit of which is a seat, from whence we have an immensely extended view of the country, and the house delightfully situated in the lawn below. It would be contrary to my plan, which is only to give the reader a general idea of this place, preparatory to his perusal of the following pages, and indeed impossible, to enumerate all the beauties that appear from this eminence. On the back of the seat is this inscription, taken from the fifth book of Paradise Lost:

Thefe are thy glorious works, Parent of good,
Almighty! thine this univerfal frame——

We shall therefore retire into the grove behind; where, from the first bench, the eye is presented with a more confined prospect, which, by its variety, is rendered doubly pleasing. Thomfon's feat, the Temple of Thefeus, and the obelisk, appear to great advantage, at well judged distances amidst hanging woods, and lawns covered with the liveliest verdure. From the second bench is seen, between the branches of the trees, the stupendous Wrekin, a high mountain in Shropshire, at the distance of at least thirty miles, and the buildings are totally excluded. The path now leads to the Doric Portico, thus inscribed,

Quieti et Mufis.

This is, in my opinion, one of the most agreeable retreats in the park; and is situated on the brow of a very steep lawn, bounded every way by the noblest trees that ever graced the forest.

From

Hence the path leads into a rude and gloomy dell, down whose deep shelving sides several little streams continually run, that delight us with their coolness, and soothe us with their murmurs.

After rising the declivity on the opposite side, the path leads to the Rotunda, a neat and elegant building, from which the alcove and water above-mentioned are very striking objects. Proceeding onward we descend into another deep glen, but in many circumstances varying from the former, and soon after the scene changes into a beautiful extent of lawn, where the parsonage-house presents itself to the view, and a graceful row of elms conducts us to Thomson's seat.

The prospect from this spot is such, as never fails to fix the attention, and raise the delight of the beholder. The steep hanging woods directly opposite; amidst which the Doric portico displays itself with greater beauty; the Clent Hills and the Ruin on one hand, with the romantic Malvern Hills bounding the horizon on the other, contribute to adorn the scene with variety, beauty, and grandeur.

Winding through the grove on the right, which affords a distant view of lord Stamford's grounds, an eminence appears, on the brow of which is erected the Column, bearing a statue of Frederic, prince of Wales, the father of his present majesty. The view from hence is equally extensive with that from the hill before-mentioned, commands the house, and is in every respect correspondent with that display of taste and magnificence, which prevails amidst the recesses of Hagley.

HAGLEY.

H A G L E Y.

O N C E more, with trembling hand, I ſtrike the lyre,
Genius of verſe the living lays inſpire;
Ye tenants of the glade, that o'er me ſpread
Your flutt'ring wings, and warble round my head,
Lend me your notes—and thou, whoſe love-lorn tale,
Wild-echoing, floats along the dying gale,
O Philomel—if e'er at eve I rove
To hear thy tender plaints in yonder grove;
O ſweeteſt far of all the feather'd train,
Warm my rapt breaſt with thy ſeraphic ſtrain:
HAGLEY I ſing—to HAGLEY's bowers belong
The ſofteſt meaſures, and the nobleſt ſong.

Ye bleſt retreats, ye pleaſing glooms, all hail!
Ye varied ſcenes of woodland, hill and dale,
Whether my eyes with hurried glance ſurvey
Yon flow'ring lawns in wild luxuriance gay,
Or to thoſe diſtant foreſts ſtretch with pain,
That tower to heav'n and darken all the plain:

Still

Still as the varied profpect meets my fight,
My confcious bofom beats with new delight.

  Where fhall the fong begin? For every place
Invites alike, and beams with rival grace:
From fcene to fcene the mufe bewilder'd flies,
While more than fairy landfcapes round her rife—
Such mingled tranfports our grand parent knew,
When nature's charms firft met his wond'ring view;
Led by his Maker thro' the blooming wild,
Where-e'er he rov'd, rekindling beauties fmil'd:
On ev'ry plant he gaz'd, on ev'ry flower,
And tafted ev'ry fruit that deck'd the bower;
Paus'd in the valley, mark'd the mountain's pride,
Or hanging o'er the fountain's verdant fide,
Admir'd his fhadow in the filver flood;
The gay reflected lawn, the dancing wood,
The heav'n's blue concave, and the folar blaze—
Till thought was loft amidft the fhining maze!

  Ye fpreading limes! On whofe majeftic brows
An hundred rolling years have fhed their fnows;
Ye hills and op'ning plains, where nature pours
With lavifh hand the choiceft of her ftores;

                                        Ye

Ye hallow'd roofs, which fcience hath array'd
In all the glowing pomp of light and fhade,
That oft have heard a Pope's melodious tongue,
And oft refounded while a Thomfon fung,
Receive the meaneft of the tuneful train,
Who trembles while he wakes the votive ftrain.
Beauty and ftrength thro' all the pile unite,
Warm the bold thought, and fix the roving fight:
Tafte guides the rule, while judgment marks the lines,
And all the mafter in the ftructure fhines.
Here live the rev'rend fages of mankind,
Whofe works delighted, or inform'd the mind;
The laurel'd offspring of immortal Rome
Live here, and with their prefence guard the dome!
Here too her later fons, not lefs in fame,
Whofe fingers wak'd to life the pencil'd frame,
Or foften'd into fenfe the rugged ftone,
Flourifh amidft creations of their own.

Come forth, my mufe, and wand'ring o'er the green,
Mark the fair glories of this living fcene—
From yon proud Obelifk, whofe tow'ring brow
Throws its long fhadows o'er the plains below;

From:

From yonder Fane*, which darkſome firs embrace,
Down to the graceful Column's humbler baſe:
O would ſome power my kindling breaſt inſpire
With Titian's genius, or with Thomſon's fire;
Soon ſhould the ſmiling lawn, the purple ſkies,
The hanging grove, on breathing canvas riſe;
In all its charms the vivid landſcape ſhine,
And nature's touches only rival mine.

Beneath this antient pile, whoſe Gothic tower
Pale ivy claſps, and circling elms embower,
Reſts his pale head, who firſt theſe beauties plann'd,
And rais'd this Eden with his foſt'ring hand—
Dumb the ſoft muſic of his tuneful tongue,
On which the liſt'ning ſwains enraptur'd hung;
That heart, which lately leapt at beauty's name,
That glow'd with virtue's, friendſhip's pureſt flame,
Beats now no more—let thoughtleſs man attend,
And mark the point where all his triumphs end!
With mournful pomp, by his unconſcious ſide,
Cold as her urn, reclines his beauteous bride;

* Temple of Theſeus.

To

To whofe fair memory flow'd the tend'reft tear,
That ever trembled o'er the female bier :
O let congenial anguifh paufe, and weep,
Where beauty, worth, and buried genius fleep !

Thou little murmuring rill fhalt be our guide,
Whofe amber waves along the pebbles glide ;
Sacred perhaps to fome fair rural power,
That fweeps unfeen amidft the neighb'ring bower. ·

To that lone Dell, beneath the deepen'd fhade,
Where down the valley burfts the rude cafcade ;
Hence let us fly from day's increafing beam,
Lull'd by the murmurs of the babbling ftream :
Or farther bend, to where the moaning dove
Invites our fteps to yonder gay Alcove :
Delightful haunt—where fportive elves repair,
And chaunt foft warblings to the midnight air;
What diftant found is that which meets my ears,
Sweet as the mufic of the rolling fpheres !
Heav'n's ! what a glorious fcene ! with rapid fweep
The headlong waters rufh from fteep to fteep ;
While the grey rocks, whofe bafe they foam around,
Repels them as they break with furious bound :

Q

The fparkling fun-beams on their furface play,
And the bright waves reflect a double day.
Mark with what pomp the dark o'er-arching wood
Bends its broad arms to tafte the billowy flood;
While far above, on yon green mountain's height.
The bold rotunda fwells upon my fight.

Now o'er the floping lawn's luxuriant fide,
Where ftands the portico in all its pride;
Soft let me feek the grotto's cool retreat,
And reft awhile on yon fequefter'd feat
Beneath that antient oak—the foreft's boaft,
Whofe branching arms might fhield a num'rous hoft—
Fair Venus, to thy guardian power I bow,
Propitious fmile, and hear my proffer'd vow;
Still on thy bard thy genial influence fhed,
Still twine thy myrtles round his favour'd head;
So fhall he wake for thee the founding ftring,
And ev'ry mountain with thy praifes ring.
Ye mofs-clad banks, where twining violets bloom,
That load the fcented breeze with foft perfume:
Ye verdant fhrubs, permit a ftranger gueft
On your foft couch his fainting limbs to reft——

Thou,

Thou gushing flood, thro' whose transparent stream,
Of glassy hue, a thousand fragments gleam,
Still murmur on—while Morpheus, drowsy god,
O'er my scorch'd temples waves his leaden rod.
But other scenes, as rapturous, bid me rise,
And other beauties call my wandering eyes.

Now will the muse the winding path ascend,
And to that gloomy bank her footsteps bend,
To hail her Shenstone—and, with grief sincere,
Drop o'er his shade the tributary tear;
That tear which he to suff'ring virtue gave,
Shall now bedew his own lamented grave.

Ye fairy vales, and thou, enchanting glade *,
His fostering hand in artless pomp array'd,
Where is your Corydon ? Ye sylvan powers,
That wont to rove 'midst those deserted bowers,
With roses who shall deck your lonely way,
What birds shall warble, or what fountains play ?
For Corydon is gone—The shepherds come,
But ev'ry flute, and ev'ry voice is dumb;

* Virgil's Grove; which is the glory of tho Leasowes.

The

The flocks with fhriller plaints his lofs deplore,
And, bleating moan—" Our mafter is no more!"

In yonder lawn, befide the bending wood,
The bard of Twit'nam erft, delighted ftood;
With nature's charms, or Homer's rapt, he fung,
And lays fpontaneous warbled from his tongue.
Behold where friendfhip rears the pious urn,
Fond pledge of thee that never muft return,
In thefe lov'd haunts, with more than mortal fire,
To fwell the notes, and fmite the founding lyre.

How high yon Turret, mouldering in decay,
Majeftic foars 'midft ruins rude and grey;
Up the fteep pile afpiring ivy creeps,
And in its fhade the bat fecurely fleeps:
Ah, Lyttelton! in vain thy fancy ftrives
To imitate, where real nature lives—
For ftill in fpite of thee, in fpite of art,
Her ancient fpirit breathes thro' ev'ry part—
In fome bleft moment, fure, thy daring hand
O'erpower'd the nymph, and caught her magic wand!
Trembling, at length, I reach the glorious height,
And the wide landfcape burfts upon my fight;

Scarce

Scarce can I roll my eyes from fide to fide,
Where far beneath the diftant rivers glide:
Where cities fwell, where forefts, dark and deep,
Stretch o'er the vallies with tremendous fweep——
Here the proud Malvern * hills remantic rife,
There the great Wrekin mingles with the fkies;
Here Clent's delightful fummits fmile around,
And the Black Mountains † there the vaft horizon bound.

Now let the notes in mournful cadence flow,
All wildly fweet, and breathe the foul of woe;
Strains, fuch as warbled late o'er Lucia's tomb,
Sooth'd her pale ghoft, and chear'd the mirky gloom:
When thefe lone bow'rs with fofter meafures rung,
Than ever dropt from Petrarch's tender tongue.
Her courfe the mufe to yonder mountain bends,
Where, wrapt in fhade, the leffening fpire afcends,
There will fhe wail the royal infant's doom,
Bid round his fhrine eternal laurels bloom;
And while her eyes pour forth the torrent flood,
Her hand fhall write the tale in lines of blood!

---

* The Malvern hills divide this county, on the fouth-weft fide, from Herefordfhire, and rife to a great height, one above another, for feven miles together.

† Thefe mountains, and the round hill near Radnor in Wales, are, in a clear atmofphere, diftinctly vifible; though at the diftance of near eighty miles.

In

In thofe dark times, when frantic difcord pour'd
The gleaming horrors of her vengeful fword
O'er half the ravag'd globe—and Saxon chains
In flavery bound Britannia's hardy fwains,
There dwelt a prince *; whom fate's fevereft frown
Curft with the hopes of Mercia's glittering crown ;
For ere nine fummers, circling o'er his head,
On his young cheek the filver down had fpread,
The haplefs Kenelm wept his ravifh'd fire,
And faw the brother of his heart expire!
Nor yet remain'd a mother's foft'ring care,
To gild the fcene, and chafe his deep defpair ;
The baleful hour that life to Kenelm gave,
Confign'd the wretched parent to the grave.

---

* " On the death of Kenulph, King of the Mercians, the kingdom fell to his fon
" Kenelm, then an infant, whofe elder fifter, Quendred, practifed with Afkebert, her lover,
" and the young king's guardian, to make away with him; which, that he might do the
" more fecretly, he had the young king into Clent-wood, in this county, under the fair pre-
" tence of taking pleafure in hunting, and when he had gotten him into a fuitable place, he
" cut off his head, and buried him where no man knew."

Vide Plott's Hift. of Staffordfhire, p. 412.

Subjects of the defcriptive kind labour under this peculiar difadvantage : they are feldom read
but by perfons who are interefted by their particular knowledge of the beauties of the place
defcribed. To make them more general therefore, by introducing hiftorical events, or enli-
vening epifodes, has been always the conduct of writers who were emulous of more univerfal
attention. If the candid reader will forgive the difproportionate length of the following ftory,
which is not the offspring of poetic invention, the author hopes the truly tragical fcenes it
contains will fufficiently apologize for its other defects.

One

One only fifter fhar'd his filial grief,
Whofe fondnefs gave his bleeding heart relief;
Forlorn they wander thro' the lonely wood,
And mix their murmurs with the founding flood;
Or fpeechlefs bend and kifs the hallow'd bier,
Returning figh for figh, and tear for tear.

Thus many a tedious month in anguifh paft,
And ev'ry month more irkfome than the laft;
But fiercer pangs the beauteous maid oppreft,
And love and grief divide her anxious breaft.
To guard the realm from foreign tyrant's rage,
And guide the monarch in his tender age,
Was Afkebert's high care; whofe mighty name,
Thro' all the weft renown'd for martial fame,
Struck dread thro' ev'ry rebel Saxon's foul,
That dar'd refift his fov'reign's high controul;
Yet beauty's charms could fmooth the warrior's brow,
His breaft of fteel with fofter trrnfports glow;
Thofe finewy limbs, that on the embattled plain
Sublimely tower'd o'er myriads of the flain,
With matchlefs grace amidft the dance could move,
And warm the tender female heart to love.

3

Fais

Fair Kendred faw, and felt the rapturous heat
Thro' ev'ry pulfe with quick vibration beat:
In vain fhe ftrove her frantic pains to hide,
Or ftop refiftlefs paffion's fwelling tide;
Her confcious thoughts in all her features rife,
Glow on her cheeks, and languifh in her eyes:
Nor lefs the baron felt the fecret flame,
But figh'd impatient for the royal dame;
Such favage joy the tiger's breaft infpires,
Or dæmons, madd'ning with inceftuous fires!
Treafon and flaughter in his bofom brood,
That burns for power, and thirfts for infant blood;
His guilty flame from curft ambition fprings,
And love conceals a dagger with his wings—
Yet fofteft founds adorn'd his flowing tongue,
On which the nymph with rapt attention hung,
Swift thro' each fenfe the mingling poifon ftole,
And fcepter'd fplendors fire her tainted foul.
Warm'd by her fmiles, the fell barbarian glows,
His dark and dreadful purpofe to difclofe;
And while with eager joy her hand he preft,
Thus his falfe lips th' attentive maid addreft:
" Faireft of Mercia's nymphs, whofe angel charms
" Have fill'd this panting breaft with foft alarms;

3

" Dear,

" Dear, blooming idol of my doating eyes,

" For whom I wafte the tedious night in fighs,

" How long in doubt and anguifh fhall I pine,

" When call that paradife of beauty mine ?

" Hafte thee, my love; to yonder fane away,

" The breathing altars chide our long delay;

" This hour the hoary feer fhall join our hands,

" And Hymen bind us in his myrtle bands."

The nymph obey'd: her kindling cheeks affume

A deeper crimfon, as fhe reach'd the dome.

There while the priefts the folemn rites prepare,

He mark'd the tumults of the trembling fair;

And gazing, with that look of villain joy,

That mafks the fiend, and fmiles—but to deftroy;

On ev'ry charm with wanton praifes dwelt,

Diffembling tranfports which he never felt:

" Bleft with the beams of thofe blue rolling eyes,

" I envy not the gods their purple fkies;

" My Kendred's thoufand beauties to behold,

" Might draw down Woden * from his throne of gold,

" But Woden's felf fhould never tafte thy charms,

" Nor force thee trembling from my bridal arms:

* Woden was the principal deity of the Saxons.

R

" How

" How would the fcepter, by thy father borne,

" His lovely daughter's fnow-white hand adorn!

" The gems, that in the crown of Mercia glow,

" How would they fparkle on thy brighter brow;

" And mingling with thy flowing, auburn hair,

" Surpafs the fplendors of the proudeft fair!

" Shake not—nor dread to mount a brother's throne,

" Which years and birth more juftly ftamp thy own;

" Infirm, and tott'ring with each rougher breeze,

" Soon may he fall the victim of difeafe;

" Or if difeafe fhould fpare his infant head,

" There want not means to mix him with the dead."—

" Ah ceafe," the Princefs cries, " that piercing ftrain,

" Nor let a fifter raife her voice in vain;

" If my lov'd Afkebert hath thus decreed,

" The throne be ours—but let not Kenelm bleed:

" O fpare his tender age, and let his fate

" Be chains for life, or exile from the ftate."

She fpake; and thus the guileful peer replied,

While his falfe tongue his murd'rous heart belied:

" Well haft thou faid—Yes, left his vengeful hand

" Hurl the red torch of faction round the land;

" Far, far from hence to Mercia's diftant bound,

" Where tracklefs forefts ftretch immenfe around,

" And

" And length'ning fwamps thro' howling defarts fpread,

" Some faithful hind his devious fteps fhall lead :

" While we, triumphing in a nation's fmile,

" The fondeft, happieft pair of Albion's ifle,

" Secure in rounds of endlefs rapture move,

" And feaft on all the luxuries of love."

The magic found fwift darted to her brain,

While fiercer tumults throb in ev'ry vein :

Her hand he printed with an ardent kifs,

And the laft rites confirm their impious blifs.

The founding clarions now th' event declare,

The affembled lords the nuptial banquet fhare;

The royal victim flew to be carefs'd,

Nor knew a *murd'rer* clafp'd him to his breaft.

" Kenelm, at length, thy pious grief refrain,

" This day demands our rapture's loudeft ftrain ;

" To-morrow mount thy choiceft, fwifteft fteed,

" Beneath our fpears the foaming boar fhall bleed :

" The youth of Mercia call thee to the plain,

" And thy fair fifter deigns to grace our train."

The prince delighted his command obeys,

And fprings from flumber with the morning rays :

But

But when the chace in all its fury burn'd,

To these lone hills his devious courfe he turn'd;

And as their fteeds the dreary wild afcend,

" This fuits our purpofe well," exclaim'd the fiend!

" Purpofe! what purpofe?—O, my honour'd lord,

" What means that frown, and ah! that gleaming fword!

" If aught my rafh, unthinking youth hath err'd,

" To rouze thy juft revenge, in deed, or word;

" Behold me roll repentant at thy feet,

" Low in the duft thy pardon to intreat;

" O, by thefe tears, that threat'ning hand remove,

" My father's friendfhip, and my fifter's love;

" In bonds of fteel my tender limbs confine,

" In damp and dreary dungeons let me pine;

" But fpare"——the brandifh'd falchion ftopt his cries,

And his meek foul fled quiv'ring to the fkies.

As the firft murd'rer, from the ftroke that gave

His proftrate, bleeding brother, to the grave;

Thus, ghaftly pale, this fecond Cain arofe,

Such horror ev'ry fhudd'ring finew froze!

But no remorfe could touch that iron heart,

Where never confcience plung'd her burning dart.

With

With favage rage his purple robes he tore,
And dy'd them deeper in the recking gore;
Then deeply delv'd the dark, unhallow'd tomb,
And gave the mangled corpfe to earth's affrighted womb.
But now, refounding from the neighb'ring vale,
The horn's fhrill clangors load the chearful gale:
Furious he fnatch'd the veft, that dropt with blood,
And, like an arrow darting thro' the wood,
Terror and guilt, wild-glaring in his eyes,
Fill'd the wild concave with his dreadful cries.
" Halt, comrades halt—this bloody robe I found
" Deep in the foreft, fmoaking on the ground;
" Some prowling favage, or fome ruffian's fword,
" Hath rent the bofom of our youthful lord;
" Through yonder brake methought I faw him borne,
" By the fierce, panting boar—all gafh'd and torn—
" Hafte, let us pierce its gloom; fome happier fpear
" May reach the monfter in his mad career."
" As mine does thee"—indignant Kendred faid,
And with her fabre clove his trait'rous head.
" The monfter thou—inhuman murderer go,
" Where vengeance waits thee in the realms below,
" To fcoffing fiends thy tale of horror tell,
" And reign with furies in the deeps of hell:

" My

" My foul with thine fhall take her guilty flight,

" Purfue thee howling thro' the realms of night;

" Still thunder in thy ears the promis'd throne,

" And make the fhades re-murmur with her moan!

" Dear, martyr'd youth, that, in thy tendereft age,

" Haft fall'n the prey of fell ambition's rage;

" On the pale, trembling wretch, from heav'n look down,

" That dared afpire to feize a brother's crown—

" Behold the proftrate author of thy woe:

" Mine was the hand that gave the deathful blow——

" Mine was the traitor-voice that bade thee bleed,

" And thus this dagger fhall revenge the deed!"

She fpake, and kiffing thrice th' impurpled veft,

Thrice plung'd the weapon in her beauteous breaft.

The mufe, all penfive, haftes to happier plains,

Where Contemplation, pale-eyed matron, reigns;

Deep thron'd in tenfold glooms that round her rife,

In proud theatric ftate, and fweep the fkies.

She comes, in robes of virgin white array'd;

Silent as night, fhe ftalks along the glade:

She fpeaks; the folemn founds conviction roll,

And rufh like lightning to my inmoft foul:

" Mortal,

" Mortal, whofe foot my hallow'd haunts pervades,

" Approach the Genius of thefe awful fhades:

" And learn—how vain the monarch's purple ftate,

" How low the boafted triumph of the great;

" Compar'd with raptures which content infpires,

" When wifdom guides the mind, and virtue fires—

" Ye blinded wretches, who for giory brave

" The battle's roar, and ftem the raging wave;

" And ye, who fir'd with boundlefs thirft of gain,

" Tempt the dark mine, or tread the burning plain,

" To this lone fpot retire, and know that " All is vain"——

But fee where gathering clouds deform the fky,

To yonder cell's deep covert let us fly,

Where darker trees their twilight horrors fpread,

And wrap fome hermit in their iron fhade—

Heard you that dreadful clap—fo loud, and long,

'Twas heav'n's high voice that ratified the fong:

Yes, ye fair fyrens, that betray mankind,

Whofe various influence tears the human mind,

Wealth, beauty, power, I dare renounce you all,

And proftrate bend at virtue's awful call!

I fee, I fee your fading charms expire,

Darken'd their luftre, and extinct their fire;

Far;

Far, far from you contented would I dwell
Beneath thefe roofs, and bid the world farewell;
Here innocence and peace fhould crown my days,
And my fond heart forget its throb for praife:
No longer confcious to the tafte of blood,
The fruits of earth fhould be my humbler food;
My thirft I'd flake in yon tranflucent ftream,
With God, my guide, my guardian, and my theme.

How foft the fragrance of this vernal fhower,
That lights the gem and wakes the drooping flower!
On magic ground, entranc'd, I feem to tread,
Where fparkling emeralds pave the glowing mead:
With more than mortal notes the groves refound,
With more than Perfian odours breathes the ground.

Ere yon refplendent lamp forfakes the day,
I'll climb the fteep, and mark his fetting ray
From yonder feat—where, to his Maker's praife,
Some pious fwain hath grav'd the duteous lays——
Unbounded fcene—beyond my humble ftrain,
For here a Milton's daring powers were vain;
" Thefe are thy glorious works, Almighty King,"
The bard aftonifh'd faid, and dropp'd the ftring!

If

If my fond eyes the diftant hills behold,
Thofe fkies, diftinct with azure and with gold,
Sweep o'er the foreft, range the defart heath,
Or wanton in the fpreading lawn beneath :
His hand I fee in nature's thoufand forms ;
His power fupports them, and his fpirit warms.

How beauteous, 'midft the gay furrounding mead,
Does yon proud manfion rear its ample head !
Whofe polifh'd towers with trembling radiance gleam,
As the broad fun obliquely darts his beam.
What tho' Dædalean fkill hath deck'd the dome,
Vandyke or Titian glow in ev'ry room;
Thefe are its meaneft pride—with all the fire,
With all the genius of his noble fire,
There dwells a Lyttelton—immortal name !
That fires my fancy with rekindling flame;
As all thy glorious anceftors I trace,
And the long fplendor of thy antient race :
Bards, Prelates, Chiefs, in bright fucceffion rife,
And ermin'd fages fweep before my eyes.

Nor will the mufe neglect, in proud difdain,
The decent village, and the lowly fwain,

The

The sheep, that thro' an hundred pastures feed,
The half-rais'd ox, and brisk disporting steed—
But ah! ye lovely, fading scenes, farewell;
Farewell ye fields, where health and pleasure dwell;
The thrush invites me from the secret bower,
The lone owl hails me from her antient tower;
The shades of eve, advancing, veil the plains,
And half unsung the pleasing theme remains.

Fatigued, tho' ravish'd with these glorious views,
Pleas'd I retire with silence and the muse
Beneath this Doric roof—my aching sight
Dwells on these humbler greens with fresh delight;
Where shades o'er shades, in deep'ning pomp, ascend,
And thro' the vale their lengthen'd gloom extend:
Here oaks of mighty growth the plain embrown,
There hoary elms or branching chesnuts frown:
Here towering limes the tempest's fury dare,
Or darker firs, luxuriant, shoot in air.

Now let me penetrate yon lonely dale,
Where in soft whispers sighs the hollow gale;
And many a murmuring rivulet breaking round,
Lulls my rapt senses with its soothing sound.

3

With

With rapture thro' the darkſome glen I ſtray,
Where twining coppice half exclude the day;
High o'er my head the cuckow ſwells her throat,
And clamorous rooks prolong the ſolemn note.
But lo, where brighter ſcenes my ſteps invite,
By change more grateful to the roving ſight;
With joy the muſe expands her riſing wing,
O'er vallies, fluſh'd with all the pride of ſpring;
O'er plains, gay-ſmiling with eternal green,
Plains, which had Mecca's boaſted prophet ſeen,
Here had he bade his blooming Houri riſe,
And HAGLEY been his fairer Paradiſe.

　The ſun hath now withdrawn his fiercer fires,
And yonder ſee his laſt, faint beam expires:
'Tis fancy's hour—and now the fairy train,
Whoſe pinions wont to ſweep the dewy plain,
Ruſh from their haunts, beneath the ſhadowy dell,
The moſs-green grotto, and the pebbled cell.
Hark! what ſoft ſtrains of muſic float around;
From bow'r to bow'r the length'ning notes refound:
Will Thomſon now deſcend and ſeize the lyre,
And join in concert with the woodland quire—

Come,

Come, gentle bard, together let us rove,
Wrapt in high converfe, thro' the darkeft grove;
Together let us tread thy fav'rite lawn,
And mark the tranfports of the bounding fawn :
For ftill, enamour'd of thy warbling fhell,
With thee, fond fwain, the Graces lov'd to dwell.
Nature confefs'd her darling's magic hand,
And flowers, obedient, fprang at thy command.
The Seafons danc'd around their bard, and fhed
Their choiceft, fweeteft products on thy head.
But nobler ftrains of bright, feraphic love,
Warm thy bold fancy in the realms above,
Delighted with fome kindred foul to ftray,
And tempt the dazzling realms of purer day.
Yet here, of old, beneath this folemn glade,
This bower, now facred to thy awful fhade;
Thou with the friendly Pope would'ft oft prolong
The focial ftrain, or raife the moral fong.
Immortal pair ! whofe lays the mufe approves,
Whom freedom honours, and their country loves.
And well might he, in whofe harmonious mind
Each fofter pow'r, and ev'ry grace combin'd,
This beauteous fcene with partial eyes furvey,
Where art and nature all their charms difplay;

Woods,

Woods, mountains, vales, with rival fplendor vie,
Awe the rapt foul, and tire the gazing eye.

The deeper fhades defcend; my anxious mufe
With quicken'd ftep the winding tract purfues:
Gloomy her path; yet oft departing day,
Thro' the long vifta darts its welcome ray:
And many an op'ning half-difplays to fight,
The dubious landfcape, fading into night.
Beyond where thofe brown defart waftes extend,
Envil's green hills and lofty woods afcend:
There Stamford, rural fwain, delights to roam,
While round the tumbling torrents dafh their foam;
Or in fome fhed of fancy's work reclines,
Sooth'd with the murmurs of his waving pines.
Great peer, ennobled by the generous mind,
Who, like the mighty fathers of mankind,
Scorns not the culture of his native plains,
Nor fpurns the labours of induftrious fwains.

Mark where the moon, in filver pomp array'd,
Skirts with her orient beam the dufky glade;
And as her filent chariot moves along,
The burning orbs of heav'n around her throng;

Full

Full on this pile her rays reflected fhine,
That bears the nobleft of the Brunfwick line.
Frederic, all hail! my country's early boaft—
O haplefs prince! admir'd, belov'd, and loft.
Thy anxious heart beat high for Britain's fame,
And Britain lov'd thee with a parent's flame.
Her daughters fung thy worth in ev'ry vale,
Her fathers pour'd the fage prophetic tale,
But heav'n forbade——and fates untimely gave
Our promis'd monarch to the barren grave!
Yet in thy fon thefe glorious lines we trace,
And all the father's virtue warms his race:
Tho' factions rouze the Britifh world to arms,
And fierce Bellona found her mad alarms,
Aw'd by the virtues of the beft of kings,
The fury fhall contract her harpy wings:
Bright from the cloud their Genius break away,
And concord fpread as boundlefs as her fway.

A

M O N O D Y,

SACRED TO THE MEMORY OF

E L I Z A B E T H,

.

DUCHESS OF NORTHUMBERLAND.

YET ONCE MORE, O! YE LAURELS—
MILTON.

A M O N O D Y,

Sacred to the Memory of ELIZABETH, Duchefs of Northumberland.

WHAT meant that plaintive, choral fwell,
That from a thoufand voices feem'd to rife,
And fpread in leffening murmurs thro' the fkies?
Big with what awful tale does yonder bell
Exalt its burial note, and pour
Its deep'ning mufic round the attentive fhore?
Smote by the hand that levels all,
Another P E R C Y dies.
But let no vulgar, impious tongue, prefume
The baleful tidings to relate,
This blackeft, bittereft ftroke of fate,
And break the eternal filence of the tomb.
The dire event a nation's cries fhould tell,
'Twas Britain's voice that wail'd her as fhe fell.
'Twas Britain's voice—and all her weeping train
Of orphans, widows mingled in the ftrain.
What monument can raptur'd fancy raife
To the fair memory of the wife and good,

T   (Tho'

(Tho' all the mufes wak'd their loftieft lays,
Tho' all the treafures of Potofi's mine
Grac'd their proud bier, and fparkled round their fhrine)
Greater than virtue's tears, and Britain's praife ?

 You fpeechlefs, pale-eyed, forrowing band,
Whofe tears and burfting fighs declare
What heart-felt pangs your bofoms tear ;
Who fhar'd her fortune, and her power,
When famine crufh'd you with his iron hand,
When death's dire harpies, burning to devour,
Difeafe and anguifh, ftalk'd around your bed,
And fhook their fcorpions o'er your frighted head ;
Oh ! Break your awful filence, and prolong
In melting rhapfodies to PERCY's name,
Your loftieft meafures,—fwell the choral fong,
Soar with her zeal, and glow with all her flame.
With flattery's arts your lays ye need not ftain,
Nor let one venal lye debafe the ftrain ;
Whate'er of daring or fublime,
The fabling fons of Phœbus dream,
To fwell the lofty rage of rhyme,
Shrinks from the grandeur of our brighter theme.
The greeneft bays that e'er the mufes fpread,
To fhade the afhes of the mighty dead,

Fade

Fade at the light of Virtue's living ray;
Where the rapt foul to nobler views afpires,
And as on eagle wing fhe breaks away,
From her frail tenèment of mould'ring clay,
Pants with diviner rage, and burns with brighter fires.

What tho' thro' thy illuftrious veins,
From many a godlike anceftor roll'd down,
And many a chief, of high renown,
That fought on Agincourt's and Creffy's plains,
The rich, patrician ftream unfullied flowed;
Though thy proud race with lengthen'd fplendours fhine,
And monarchs mingle in the mighty line,
Thefe were but humbleft trophies to thy name;
Had not thy fpirit caught the kindred flame,
Had not thy breaft with rival virtue glow'd.

Beneath thy fmiles reviving fcience rear'd
With fairer luftre her immortal head,
The fons of genius hail'd thy bounteous hand,
That oft the night of black misfortune chear'd;
And every nobler art its influence fpread,
In wider circles, round a favour'd land.

T 2

Rife,

Rife, * thou dear child of Fancy and the Nine,
Whom Nature, at thy awful birth endow'd
With rage to foar beyond the rhyming crowd;
And kindled in thy breaft the fpark divine,
That flafh'd refiftlefs thro' thy rapid line;
O! torn for ever from our longing eyes,
Whom all Parnafius widow'd fprings,
And all Caftalia's weeping grottoes mourn,
From the cold cyprefs bowers of death arife,
And feize once more thy flumbering lyre,
And deeply fmite its magic ftrings!
Let gratitude a nobler fong infpire,
Than burft, with facred energy of found,
When Cambria's cliffs, and Conway's liftening tide,
Heard their hoar prophet raife his thundering ftrain,
To blaft the tyrant Edward's banner'd pride;
Whofe ftreaming hands, with wanton vengeance red,
Reek'd with the blood of bards unjuftly flain.
His powerful verfe hath broke the fpell of death:
Mark where, flow-rifing from their rocky bed,
In ftoles of white the bearded fpectres rife,
And fcud like lightning o'er the defart heath,
And point their hoftile torches at his head.

* This alludes to a particular inftance of kindnefs fhewn by her Grace to the late Mr. Gray.

Such

Such deathlefs ftrains to PERCY's memory raife,
And let thy wild harp labour in her praife.
O could they burft death's adamantine chain,
And give her to the weeping world again !
Thy pencil's animated touch alone
Can draw the living portrait of her mind ;
Where ev'ry gentle female grace combin'd,
Where ev'ry gen'rous manly virtue fhone ;
As thou who fhar'd her bounty beft can tell,
That rais'd her name as much above her kind,
As thy bold lays each meaner mufe excel.

Ye who by birth or fortune's varying.fmile
Diftinguifh'd fhine, the guardians of our ifle;
Whether ye fwell the Senate's awful band,
Where Lyttelton, in thoughts fublime and ftrong,
Rolls the full ftream of eloquence along—
Or high on glory's glittering fummits ftand
Where all the virtues dart their blended rays,
Diffufing round the throne their central blaze;
And guide the fcepter of fupreme command;
O dare to emulate your fov'reign's zeal,
In truth's, in wifdom's caufe with PERCY glow :
Thefe are the bafis of a nation's weal,
From thefe renown and lafting tranfport flow—

Hafte

Hafte to the couch where drooping merit pines,
Where pale difeafe the languid head reclines;
Bid laurels round the brow of genius bloom,
And fnatch expiring virtue from the tomb.

Fain would the mufe each generous deed rehearfe,
And bid them flourifh in immortal verfe :
To lateft times difplay thy virtuous fame,
Till wondering ages kindle at thy name :
With all thy fpirit warm the glowing line,
Mark how the patriot, how the Chriftian fhine;
Trace thee thro' each fond fcene of private life,
In all the tender names of friend and wife;
Paint thee in ev'ry milder charm confefs'd,
And all the parent burning in thy breaft :
But what exhauftlefs toil can number o'er
The fands that fwell the deep's extended fhore,
Or in the defart waftes of Lybia rife,
When dufky whirlwinds fweep along the fkies;
And what bold tongue fhall e'er refound
The boundlefs tale of thy exalted worth,
That brightening every objeft round,
Shot forth its beams confpicuous as thy birth :

Nor

Nor did thofe beams with partial fplendor fall,

But like the fource of light, they fhone on all.

Daughters of Jove, your mournful lays forbear;

Some fong of magic virtue dare,

To chafe the fullen blacknefs of defpair,

And footh the grief-ftruck partner of her bed:

Whofe inexpreffive forrows flow,

In all the fpeechlefs agony of woe,

O'er the cold afhes of the unconfcious dead,

From the rich treafures of your tuneful art,

Some foft medicinal balm prepare,

Sweeter than all the breathing gums that fhed

Their wanton fragrance thro' Arabian air,

To heal the anguifh of his bleeding heart.

To kindred worth fweep all your warbling lyres,

O wake fome tender, thrilling, dying ftrain;

Till rapture trembles from the quivering wires,

And fofter anguifh throbs thro' every vein:

Then, as each ruder paffion finks to reft,

With fcenes of martial ardor warm his breaft,

And point his wondering eye to yonder plain;

Where in infulted Britain's glorious caufe,

His dauntlefs fon * the fword of juftice draws:

* Earl Percy; then ferving in America.

And

And as his great forefathers tower'd in arms,
Pants in the midft of battle's fierce alarms,
With eager hope to gain the glittering prize,
Which glory holds to valour's ravifh'd view:
Their lightning-terrors kindle in his eyes,
And in his breaft their ardors blaze anew.

'Tis done ;—and lo! the mitred prelate ftands,
The facred volume trembling in his hands,
The laft fad obfequies prepar'd to pay,
As the deep chorus chaunt the according lay,
And render to the ravenous grave,
That yawns to clafp her in its cold embrace,
What erft to crowded courts their luftre gave,
The boaft at once and pattern of her race.
Grandeur approach, this awful fpot furvey,
And learn a leffon from the fhrouded dead;
The rolling years urge on thy fwift decay,
And thou fhalt flumber on the fame cold bed.—
Ha! doft thou fhudder at the awful tale?
Does thy lip quiver, and thy cheek turn pale?
Or fay, do glory's charms thy thoughts beguile?
Does beauty lull thee with her fofter fmile?

Yet

Yet know,—and let thefe founds like thunder roll
Thro' all the deep receffes of thy foul;
The fparkling eyes in death fhall quench their fire,
And all thy fplendors in the duft expire.

Mark where, attended by the myriad throng,
That anxious prefs around the mournful bier,
Unable to reftrain the ftarting tear,
Death's awful train in filence move along :
Pale-glimmering torches thro' the dufky air,
On every face their funeral fplendors glare,
And kindle in the fkies a milder day,
As to yon dome * they bend their dreary way,
That rears its Gothic towers, fo fteep and hoar;
Where Britain's nobles ftrew the facred floor,
And monarchs moulder with their kindred clay.
But hark ! the loud infpiring organ blows,
And pours its labour'd harmony around !
From their eternal thrones of light,
Studded with burning fapphires bright,
Defcending feraphs propagate the found,

* Weftminfter-Abbey.

U

And fwell with tranfports of celeftial love:

Her purer fpirit mingling in their train,

Diffolves in ecftacies unknown before;

Then feeks with them a happier, brighter fhore:

On lightning pinions cleaves yon fpangled plain,

And glows for ever in the quires above.

A BRIEF

A FREE

TRANSLATION

OF THE

OEDIPUS TYRANNUS

OF

SOPHOCLES.

P R E F A C E.

THE Tragedy of which I have attempted to convey the beauties into the Englifh language in a free tranflation, ftands amidft the foremoft of the claffical productions of antiquity. Of tragical writing it has ever been efteemed the model and the mafter-piece. The grandeur of the fubject is not lefs eminent than the dignity of the perfonages who are employed in it; and the defign of the whole can only be rivalled by that art with which the particular parts are conducted. The fubject is a nation labouring under calamities of the moft dreadful and portentous kind; and the leading character is a wife and mighty prince, expiating by his punifhment the involuntary crimes of which thofe calamities were the effect. The defign is of the moft interefting and important nature, to inculcate a due moderation in our paffions, and an implicit obedience to that providence of which the decrees are equally unknown and irrefiftable.

So fublime a compofition could not fail to fecure the applaufe, and fix the admiration of ages. The philofopher is exercifed in the contemplation of its deep and awful morality; the critic is captivated by its dramatic beauties, and the man of feeling is interefted by thofe ftrokes of genuine paffion which prevail in almoft every page—which every character excites, and every new event tends to diverfify in kind or in degree.

The

The three grand unities of time, place, and action, are obferved with fcrupulous exactnefs. However complicate its various parts may on the firft view appear, on a nearer and more accurate examination we find every thing ufeful, every thing neceffary; fome fecret fpring of action laid open, fome momentous truth inculcated, or fome important end promoted: not one fcene is fuperfluous, nor is there one Epifode that could be retrenched. The fucceffive circumftances of the play arife gradually and naturally one out of the other, and are connected with fuch inimitable judgment, that if the fmalleft part were taken away the whole would fall to the ground. The principal objection to this tragedy is, that the punifhment of Oedipus is much more than adequate to his crimes: that his crimes are only the effect of his ignorance, and that confequently the guilt of them is to be imputed not to Oedipus, but Apollo, who ordained and predicted them, and that he is only *Phœbi reus*, as Seneca exprefles himfelf. In vindication of Sophocles, it muft be confidered that the conduct of Oedipus is by no means fo irreproachable as fome have contended: for though his public character is delineated as that of a good king, anxious for the welfare of his fubjects, and ardent in his endeavours to appeafe the gods by incenfe and fupplication, yet we find him in private life choleric, haughty, inquifitive; impatient of controul, and impetuous in refentment. His character, even as a king, is not free from the imputation of imprudence, and our opinion of his piety is greatly invalidated by his contemptuous treatment of the wife, the benevolent, the facred Tirefias. The rules of tragic art fcarcely permit that a perfectly virtuous man fhould be loaded with misfortunes. Had Sophocles prefented to our view a character lefs debafed by vice, or more exalted by virtue, the end of his performance would have been fruftrated; inftead of ago-

nizing

nizing compaſſion, he would have raiſed in us indignation unmixed, and horror unabated. The intention of the poet would have been yet more fruſtrated on the return of our reaſon, and our indignation would have been transferred from Oedipus to the gods themſelves—from Oedipus, who committed parricide, to the gods who firſt ordained, and then puniſhed it. By making him criminal in a ſmall degree, and miſerable in a very great one, by inveſting him with ſome excellent qualities, and ſome imperfections, he at once inclines us to pity and to condemn. His obſtinacy darkens the luſtre of his other virtues; it aggravates his impiety, and almoſt juſtifies his ſufferings. This is the doctrine of Ariſtotle and of nature, and ſhews Sophocles to have had an intimate knowledge of the human heart, and the ſprings by which it is actuated. That his crimes and puniſhment ſtill ſeem diſproportionate, is not to be imputed as a fault to Sophocles, who proceeded only on the antient and popular notion of Deſtiny; which we know to have been the baſis of Pagan theology.

It is not the intention of the Tranſlator to proceed farther in a critical diſcuſſion of the beauties and defects of a Tragedy which hath already employed the pens of the moſt diſtinguiſhed commentators; which hath wearied conjecture, and exhauſted all the arts of unneceſſary and unprofitable defence. The Tranſlator is no ſtranger to the merits of Dr. Franklin; whoſe character he reveres, and by whoſe excellent performance he has been animated and inſtructed. He thinks it neceſſary to diſclaim every idea of rivalſhip with an author of ſuch eſtabliſhed and exalted reputation. The preſent tranſlation, though it be executed with far leſs ability than that of Doctor Franklin, may deſerve ſome notice, becauſe

professedly

profeſſedly written on very different principles. The Doctor was induced by his plan, and enabled by his erudition, to encounter all the difficulties of *literal* tranſlation. This work will be found by the reader, what it is called by the writer, a *free* tranſlation. The Author was not fettered by his text, but guided by it; he has however not forgotten the boundaries by which liberal tranſlation is diſtinguiſhed from that which is wild and licentious. He has always endeavoured to reprefent the fenſe of his original, he hopes fometimes to have caught its ſpirit, and he throws himſelf without reluctance, but not without diffidence, on the candour of thoſe readers who underſtand and feel the difference that ſubſiſts between the Greek and Engliſh languages, between antient and modern manners, between nature and refinement, between a Sophocles who appeals to poſterity, and a writer who catches at the capricious taſte of the day.

THE ARGUMENT.

Oedipus, *the supposed son of* Polybus, *king of* Corinth, *leaves the palace of his father upon a reflection thrown on his birth by a courtier, to consult the oracle at* Delphi *concerning his parents. In his journey he meets* Laius, *king of* Thebes, *his real father, but unknown to him, in a narrow avenue, and being opposed by him, kills him and his attendants. He afterwards solves the riddle of the Sphynx, a monster that laid the country of* Thebes *waste with her ravages, and, as his reward, is promoted to the throne, vacant by the death of* Laius, *and to the bed of* Jocasta, *his own mother. A dreadful pestilence rages among the* Thebans, *and,* Creon *being sent to consult the oracle, brings back this answer.* "That, when they shall have banished the murderer of Laius, then resident among them, the plague should cease." Oedipus, *anxious to discover the offender, and to revenge his death, denounces the most solemn curses both against the culprit and those who conceal him. After variety of investigation,* Oedipus *himself is discovered to be the murderer. In his rage he tears out his eyes, and* Jocasta, *unable to bear the reflection of her impurity, destroys herself.*

DRAMATIS PERSONÆ.

Oedipus,			King of Thebes.
Jocafta,			Wife of Oedipus.
Creon,		-	Brother to Jocafta.
Tirefias,	-		A blind Prophet of Thebes.

Corinthian Shepherd.

Shepherd formerly belonging to Laius.

Meſſenger.

High Prieſt of Jupiter.

C H O R U S.   Confiſting of the Prieſts and antient Men of Thebes,
Theban Youths and Children of Oedipus.

S C E N E, The Area before the Palace of Oedipus; where the
Prieſts are aſſembled before the Altars,

OEDIPUS

OEDIPUS TYRANNUS.

ACT I.

Oedipus, the Priest, Creon, Chorus.

Oedipus.

Offspring of antient Cadmus, wherefore thus
With fuppliant branches prefs you round our palace?
The temples fmoak with incenfe, all our ftreets
Refound with mournful pæans, and with burfts
Of frantic woe——Behold your prince himfelf,
Ev'n Oedipus, by ev'ry tongue renown'd,
Anxious, impatient, haftes to learn the caufe
Of thefe commotions: Say, thou rev'rend feer,
Whofe years and wifdom claim my firft regard,
Say, what difafters, what unfeen diftrefs
Involve my people: have the wrathful gods
Pour'd down their vengeance for fome hidden crime,
Or hath fome plunderer laid your city wafte?
Say, for this arm fhall yield you from his rage,

Or

Or added incenfe foothe offended Jove.

Steel'd were this heart, and ill fhould I deferve

To wear the crown a grateful nation gave,

Did I not fympathize in all their griefs,

And rifk my life and fafety for their welfare.

 PRIEST. Prince of this wretched land, thine eyes behold

What proftrate throngs around thy altars poured,

Implore thy fuccour from the jaws of death.

Her unfledg'd * infant train their feeble hands

Here fuppliant ftretch; there bend her chofen youth

Renown'd in war—the venerable race

To thefe fucceed, who guard our facred rites,

Hoary with age and grief: the prieft of Jove

Bows proftrate at thy feet: O king, attend

Thy fubjects cries, who rufh in gathering throngs

To where the temples of Minerva † rife,

And where Ifmenus her prophetic ftream

Rolls by Apollo's fhrine: their facred boughs

Waving in air and weary heav'n with plaints.

---

 * The words in the original are : οὐδέ πω μακρὰν πτίσϑαι σϑένοντες; literally, not able to fly a long way.

 † In Thebes there were two temples of Pallas; one in honour of Minerva the affifter; the other in honour of the Ifmenian Minerva.

* Our ancient city, like a shatter'd wreck,

When all the fury of the tempest rages,

Sinks in the flood that swells to overwhelm her.

A savage pestilence with horrid strides

Stalks thro' our streets, and rushing from the skies

Avenging Phœbus scatters o'er the land

His burning arrows, while the gloomy grave,

Enrich'd with groans and death, exults to view

Such myriads croud his desolate domain.

Parch'd by the blast the ripening harvest dies,

Our fields are strewn with putrid carcases

That lie unburied, and still wider spread

The foul contagion : dismal screams are heard

Of women labouring with untimely birth,

Who curse the monstrous product of their womb.

O second only to the immortal gods

In wisdom and in might, extend thy arm

To save our sinking race; arise, O prince,

Shine forth, as when thy glorious presence burst

The sphynx's dark ænigma, and releas'd

---

* This comparison of a state, struggling under calamity, to a ship in distress, is to be met with in many both of the Greek and Roman classics ; it occurs again in the speech of Jocasta at the opening of the third act, or what the critics call so, for this division into acts was unknown to the Grecian stage.

From death and fervitude our drooping foul,
To life, to health and fafety—prince, to thee
We raife our anxious eyes; once more be call'd
The faviour of our race: in this dark hour,
If thy prophetic fkill may ought avail :
For oft the counfels of the wife avert
The threaten'd ill. Let not oblivion fhade
Thy former godlike deeds. This city ftands
The great recording herald of thy fame :
Act like thyfelf; and know, illuftrious fire,
A kingdom's ftrength confifts not in extent
Of vaft domains, and bulwarks rais'd to heav'n;
The people are its ftrength, and when thefe fail,
Its fleets are ufelefs, and its bulwarks vain.

   Oed. Alas! my fons, ye urge not your complaints
Unknown or unregarded; well I know
The various labours that opprefs the ftate :
Nor hath your fov'reign borne amidft you all
The flighteft fhare of woe. Still have I felt
For every pang the meaneft fubject knows.
This breaft, where all your cares a center find,
Feels no repofe, but bears an empire's toils.
Whether by night upon my couch I lie,

                          Or

Or thron'd in regal pomp.   All-feeing Jove,

Witnefs the tears I fhed, the fighs I pour.

How rove my thoughts in mazy wand'rings loft,

Some med'cine to explore for bleeding Thebes.

What prudence bade I fail'd not to perform

With early fpeed: to Delphi's fhrine I fent

Creon, my noble relative and friend,

To feek of Jove, what dark unpurg'd offence

Hath ftain'd the land; what offering may atone,

And mitigate the wrath of angry Heav'n.

My foul is big with terror while I wait

The God's decree: the time of his return

Is near elaps'd, and may the curfe be mine

If I not execute in all its force

The dread beheft.

   PRIEST.   Aufpicious are thy words;

Thefe youths pronounce, that Creon is arriv'd.

  OED.   O great Apollo! Grant his chearful looks

Be the fair omen of thy fmile reftor'd.

  PRIEST.   Thus may we well divine, for bright indeed

His afpect; and around his temples wave

The joyful laurels †.

   OED.   What his tidings, foon

---

† When the perfon, who was fent to confult the oracle, returned crowned with laurel, it was a fign of his having received a favourable anfwer.

He

He will himself unfold; illustrious prince,
What answer bear'st thou from the shrines of Delphi?

CRE.   Most happy, if the voice of wisdom guide
The sons of Thebes: the storm that now impends,
Threat'ning her overthrow, will soon subside.

OED.   Mysterious are thy words; my anxious mind
Fluctuates 'midst doubt and terror.

                              CRE.   If my liege
Command me to declare the will of Jove,
Before this great assembly, I obey:
Or in the private chambers of the palace,
Submissive wait his will.

                    OED.   Declare aloud
The sov'rain will: for know, my peoples grief
Oppress me more than all my private woes.

CRE.   Reveal'd shall be the whole—The God comr
To drive from out our land the baleful source
Of these our sufferings; nor to nourish more
A wretch, accurst by all the pow'rs of Heav'n.

OED.   What wretch?—declare, how shall we soothe his ra̤

CRE.   Let banishment, or instant death arrest
His guilty steps; 'tis blood, 'tis blood, my friends,

                                        A murder'd

A murder'd king's unexpiated blood,

Hath laid our country wafte.

    OED. Whofe blood? Explain

This hideous myftery!

   CRE. Know, illuftrious prince,

Ere thou waft feated on the throne of Thebes,

Laïus our monarch held the reins of empire.

 OED. Report hath told me fo; I knew him not.

 CRE. This prince unjuftly flain, the pow'rs above

Command us to avenge, and drag to light

The bafe affaffins.

    OED. Ha! where lurk the traitors?

How fhall we trace this foul and murd'rous deed

To its dark fource?—but fay, where fell the prince?

 CRE. In this fame land he fell; let guards be fent

T' explore the country, left he 'fcape by flight:

Our early vigilance may fave an empire.

 OED. Declare the time, and manner of his death;

Each circumftance recall to mind; in Thebes

Met he this fate, or in a foreign land?

 CRE. He went (as was reported) to confult

Some diftant oracle, but ne'er return'd

To fill his vacant throne.

   OED. But did no flave,

Y

No

No meſſenger of all his train return,
To ſpread theſe tidings of your ſov'reign's death ?

CRE. One only 'ſcap'd by flight, the reſt all fell,
Amidſt the general ſlaughter : him his fright
Permitted but in memory to retain
One trivial circumſtance.

OED. Say, what was that ?
One glimmering ſpark may light us on our way
Thro' all this maze of guilt.

CRE. That robbers ſlew him :
He fell not by a ſingle ruffian's hand,
But by the power of multitudes combin'd.

OED. How could a band of robbers dare a deed,
So perilous ?

CRE. Such were our ſurmizes then :
But thus unaided, unaveng'd, expir'd
The beſt of princes.

OED. Wherefore pried you not
Into this dark event with keener ſearch ?

CRE. 'Twas then the monſter Sphinx to Thebes propoſed
Her dire ænigma, and remoter cares
Were buried in the ſenſe of preſent ills.

OED. Mine be the care ; our grateful vows we pay,

First

First to * all-feeing Phœbus; next to thee,

O prince, the warmest thanks of Thebes are due.

Hence with your fears, your Oedipus once more

Will stand the bulwark of your falling state.

This arm shall drag the traitor from his covert ;

Not only for the sake of you, my friends,

And this your murder'd sov'reign, but my own.

Soon may the daring regicides attempt

To murder me, my children, or my queen.

Arise my sons, and henceforth throw aside

Your suppliant boughs.   Before these glowing altars

Let heralds summon all the race of Cadmus.

Phœbus our guide, together will we raise

Our heads triumphant, or together sink

In undistinguish'd ruin.

   PRIEST.   Yes, my sons,

Arise, since thus our monarch hath resolv'd :

May that immortal power, whose awful voice

Utter'd the prophecy descend from Heav'n,

Avenge our cause, and save expiring The bs.

   * Sol, qui terrarum flammas opera omnia lustras.

C H O R U S.
S T R O P H E I.

Immortal, high, harmonious ſtrain!

That arm'd with awful terrors from above,

    Didſt break from Delphi's golden fane,

Bearing to Thebes the dread command of Jove:

Thy ſounds with terror fill my anxious breaſt.

    To thee our ſorrowing pæans riſe,

Patron and parent of the healing art.

    Delian, O quickly cleave the ſkies.

Arm'd with thy quiver, thy unerring dart,

And purge our city from this raging peſt.

A N T I S T R O P H E I.

Daughter of hope, fair child of light,

What great events in time's dark womb conceal'd,

    Are now emerging to our ſight;

Or wait the rolling hours to be reveal'd?

Thee, Pallas, thee, the guardian of our land,

    We firſt invoke, and thee, whoſe ſhrine,

Fills our extended forum's ample ſpace,

    With theſe thine aid far-darting Phœbus join:

Haſte, haſte, auſpicious, to our ſinking race;

Pierce the dark fiend, and ſtay his waſteful hand.

STROPHE

S T R O P H E II.

The pride of Thebes is levell'd with the ground,

    The fruits of earth lie blafted on the plain :

Her palaces with fhrieks of death refound,

    And her ftreets groan beneath the heaps of flain.

So wide hath fpread the monfter's fiery rage,

Beauty's flufh'd cheek with fatal crimfon burns ;

    From her wild eye pernicious lightning glares :

E'vn virtue's hallow'd plaint the tyrant fpurns ;

    The fcreaming infant from the bofom tears,

And ftrikes to earth the hoary fcalp of age.

A N T I S T R O P H E II.

The mother with convulfive tortures torn,

    Faints 'midft her pains, and languifhes in death.

Her haplefs infant curft as foon as born,

    Imbibes pollution with his earlieft breath.

But hark ! in louder burfts the pæans break ;

The fhores will wilder acclamations ring,]

    Mad with the flames that revel thro' their blood.

Increafing throngs around our altars cling,

And fwift as rapid fire, or torrent flood,

    By myriads rufh to Lethe's gloomy lake.

STROPHE III.

Bright offspring of the thunderer hear;
Hear Pallas, from thy central throne of light,
Seize thy dread shield, thy mighty spear,
And hither, O! direct thy rapid flight.
Enthron'd on high, with ruin by his side,
This ravager, who spurns the mail of war,
Hath slain thy people, and thy groves defil'd.
O! dash him from his fiery car,
Drive him far hence to Scythia's rocky wild,
Or deep ingulph him in the Thracian tide.

ANTISTROPHE III.

But chief, dread ruler of the skies,
Dare thou thine arm, with keener lightnings red,
Omnipotent! in vengeance rise,
And let those lightnings blast his impious head.
Monarch of Lydia, stretch thy mighty hand,
Bid thy unconquer'd shafts the monster rend;
O thou, whose darts Lyceum's summits fire,
O Bacchus, crown'd with chaplets, hither bend——
Bacchus, who lov'st to join the madd'ning quire,
Rush on th' accursed * god, and drive him from the land.

* Ἀπότιμον ἐν θεοῖς θεόν.
A god accurst among the gods.

ACT II.

OEDIPUS, CHORUS, TIRESIAS.

Θ.

OEDIPUS.

WHATE'ER my fubjects juftly can demand,
To grant is my ambition : therefore hear
My words obedient ;. fo fhall we obtain
Relief from heav'n, and expiate our offence.
I knew not 'till this day the dire event,
Not ev'n report had told me ; but there feem
Some fure, tho' fecret traces, that may lead
To full detection of this monftrous crime.
Hear then this laft refolve, which I, your king,
(Who glory in the name of citizen)
To all the citizens of ample Thebes
Aloud proclaim.   If any fubject know
By whom the fon of Labdacus was flain,
'Tis my command that inftant he reveal
The fatal fecret : let not dread of death
Reftrain him, for the murd'rer fhall not die :
His exile fhall alone fuffice to pay

I

The debt of vengeance; if by foreign hand
His blood was fpilt, whoever brings to light
The traiterous parricide the fons of Thebes
With lavifh honours fhall reward his zeal.
But if, from friendfhip, or whatever caufe,
He fcreen the murderer, let him ponder well
His dreadful doom. We further then command
That none thro' all our wide domain receive
A monfter fo defil'd : that none hold converfe,
In word or action, with him : drive him out
From all your temples : let him not approach
Your folemn facrifices, nor partake
The facred fprinklings : but purfue, purfue,
With loudeft execrations thro' the land
The univerfal peft : this awful curfe
The god of Delphi thunders on his head.
If fome bold ruffian fingly dar'd the deed,
Or leagued with numbers, be they ftill accurft;
May poverty exhauft their weary lives;
The fports of pain, and victims of difeafe!
If in this palace I conceal the traitor,
Show'r down, ye heav'ns, thefe curfes on the head
Of Oedipus, and all his perjur'd race.

'Tis

Not heav'n alone, the virtues of your king
Command this tribute; I am bound to pay
The debt of ample juftice to his manes.
I, who enjoy his fcepter and his bed,
And, had not unrelenting fate oppos'd
His fond defires, had fhar'd his * children too——
Urg'd by a fon's regard, I will avenge
This beft of princes: fmile ye mighty names
That laid the bafis of this tow'ring empire,
Cadmus, Agenor, for I *will* avenge
The blood of your defcendant. Are there yet,
Among the fons of Thebes, who wifh to fcreen
So bafe a parricide: thou parent earth,
Ope not the treafures of thy fruitful womb
To this ungrateful race: curft be their beds,
And barren; curft the produce of their toil,
'Till the fame fate fhall crufh their impious heads.
Juftice divine, and ye immortal powers
Who guard the innocent, affift our caufe,
The caufe of virtue and of injur'd kings.

   CHOR. Prince, may each curfe thy lips have now pronounced,
Alight on me, if, confcious to the fact,
I fcreen the murderer, or abet his caufe.

---

  * The introduction of this circumftance has a ftriking effect : Laius had a child, and that child was Oedipus; though his being expofed was kept as fecret as his birth.

But

But the bright power, who utter'd the decree,
Can best explain its meaning.

     OED. Just, O sage:
But if the god incline not to reveal it,
Who shall extort the secret from a power
Arm'd with omnipotence?

     CHOR. Will then my liege
Attend an old man's counsel?

     OED. Speak, if aught
Thy mind conceives, of import to the state.

 CHO. In wisdom equall'd by the gods alone,
The hoary seer, Tiresias, may unfold·
Its hidden purport.

    OED. Creon thus advised;
And messengers have twice been sent to summon
The rev'rend prophet; at his strange delay
I wonder much.

   CHO. 'Tis well; for other tales,
Various and vague are rumour'd of his death.

 OED. What are they, say? For I should know them all
To judge aright.

   CHO. They say the prince was slain
By travellers.

   OED. This hath likewise reach'd my ears;
But who hath yet appear'd to prove the fact?

            CHO.

Cho. If he exift on earth, thy menaces
Will force the confcious villain to confefs.

Oed. Whoever dar'd the execrable deed
Will not be ftartled at the impending curfe.

Cho. But this way, lo! they lead the holy feer,
Who can alone difclofe the fatal truth.

Oed. All-wife Tirefias! Thou, whofe mighty mind
Can pierce the dark, myfterious depths of fate,
Whatever in the womb of night, unborn,
Or what, amidft the great decrees of heav'n,
Lies hid from mortal ken: tho' dim the rays
Of outward fight, yet well thy mental eye
Beholds the toils of Thebes, whofe anxious fons
Call thee to be their faviour: for when late
We fought at Delphi's fhrine the will of Jove,
Thus fpake the eternal voice: " With inftant death
" Or everlafting exile, fine the wretch
" That murder'd Laius: this command obey'd,
" The plague fhall ceafe to defolate your land."
O! therefore, if thy fage, prophetic fkill,
From birds or ominous figns can ought divine,
From fwift deftruction fnatch thyfelf and Thebes;
Avenge a murder'd prince; and thy reward
Reap in a nation's pray'rs, and thofe pure joys

The

The virtuous feel, in aiding the diftreft.

Tir. How fatal knowledge proves, when thus to know
Is to be doubly wretched! when, to fpeak,
And to be filent, tire alike the fource
Of bittereft grief! O had I ne'er approach'd——

Oed. What dreadful fecret labours in thy breaft,
Darkening thy brow?

Tires. Difmifs me from thy prefence;
Thy future peace and mine depend upon it.

Oed. 'Twere bafe ingratitude to Thebes, who bore
And nourifh'd thee, to hide the will of Jove
At this dread crifis.

Tires. Rafh, rafh prince, forbear,
Left I too fuddenly that will difclofe.

Oed. O by the gods reveal it, if thou know'ft;
Suppliant we all befeech thee.

Tires. Urge no more
The knowledge of thofe woes that, ah! too foon
Will burft upon thee.

Oed. How? Know'ft thou our fate,
Yet feal'ft thy lip in filence; thus betraying
Thy prince and country?

Tires. Yes, my lips are feal'd:

Beware

Beware thy bafe fufpicions tempt me not
To break that filence.

    OED. I can hold no longer.
Traitor, fince thou art deaf to our intreaties,
Thou fhalt reveal it, for I'll force it from thee.

  TIRES. Thou blame'ft my conduct; heedlefs that thy own
Ungovernable temper leaft becomes
This facred place.

    OED. Who can reftrain his rage,
That fees thee treat, with infolent contempt,
A nation's cries?

    TIRES. What, on the book of fate,
The hand of Jove hath grav'd, fhall come to pafs,
Tho' I remain in everlafting filence.

  OED. But duty to thy country calls upon thee
To fpeak her doom.

    TIRES. Still let thy tongue rail on;
Thy fierceft rage fhall never tear it from me.

  OED. I then will fpeak—for if aright I judge,
Thyfelf wert confcious to this deed of horror:
Nay, had thine eyes retain'd their light, I think,
Wouldft with thine own bafe hand have done it too.

  TIRES. Hear me, proud prince—the curfe thou haft pronounc'd
On thine own head recoils: murd'rer, avaunt——
For from this day, this day of thy difgrace,

              The

The meaneſt ſlave ſhall ſpurn thee as profane,

Accurſt by heav'n, and ſacred to its rage.

OED. Miſcreant, and hop'ſt thou for this daring inſult

To go unſcourg'd?

TIRES. Tyrant, I ſcorn thy threats;

Truth is my fortreſs, and, againſt thy power,

Girds me, as with a coat of adamant.

OED. But tell me from what ſource thy knowledge ſprings

From thy prophetic art?

TIRES. Nay, from thyſelf:

Thy haughty treatment forced me to reveal it.

OED. Once more then with the ſound refreſh my ſoul.

TIRES. Wilt thou provoke me farther; was my meaning

Hid in ambiguous phraſe?

OED. Nay, but repeat

Thy wonderous tale.

TIRES. I tell thee then again,

Thou art that wretch, that murderer whom thou ſeek'ſt——

OED. By heav'ns, thou ſhalt not twice inſult thy prince

And go unpuniſh'd.

TIRES. Should I tell thee more,

How would'ſt thou madden!

OED. Speak it all, for all

Is one rank forgery.

TIRES. Know, unholy fires

Within that foul, unconfcious bofom burn :
Nor heed'ft thou that the partner of thy joys
Shall prove ere long the fource of all thy woes.

OED.   Still fhall thy tongue fpit forth its dark abufe
Againft thy fovereign.

TIRES.   I regard thee not,
While truth remains my fhield.

OED.   Traitor, thou ly'ft——
Truth never harbour'd in fo bafe a foul;
Blacken'd by every crime, and like thy form
Involv'd in total night.

TIRES.   Beware the taunt,
That foon, with triple force, fhall fall on thee.

OED.   Thy blindnefs is thy fafeguard, or long fince
This arm had punifh'd thy abufe with death.

TIRES.   Still I defy thee, for thy murderous fword
Shall never drink my blood—The gods protect me.

OED.   Was this bafe falfehood forg'd by thee or Creon?

TIRES.   By neither; as thy fate too foon fhall prove.

OED.   Painful pre-eminence of wealth and power,
And wifdom, laft, beft, nobleft gift of heav'n !
Since envy thus purfues to blaft the fteps
Of all that's fair or excellent on earth :
This crown, unfought by me, which grateful Thebes

Placed

Placed on my brow, that bafeft of mankind,

Creon, Whom late I deem'd my firmeft friend,

Would ravifh from me, and hath here fuborn'd

This curft magician, this vile fon of fraud,

This wily, wand'ring, fubtle hypocrite,

This bafe impoftor, * blind to ev'ry fenfe

But that of gain, with crimes of blackeft die

To load my name, and fully all my glory!

Tell me, thou vaunting prophet, where waft thou

When the fell Sphynx her dark myfterious fong

Propos'd to Thebes: fpeak, dotard, for to folve

Her dire ænigma, afk'd methinks at leaft

A prophet's pow'r——Then Oedipus arofe,

And, without aid of dreams, or auguries,

But by the native vigour of a foul

That pierces thine, and Creon's dark defigns,

Whofe bold ambition aims to feize my crown,

Solv'd the dire riddle----but beware, impoftor,

Thou and thy traitor friend, I fay, beware!

Or dearly ye fhall rue the wild attempt.

And did not years proteƈt thee from my rage,

I fhould, ere now, have taught thee not to rouze

The wrath of kings.

        Cho. If to decide be mine,

* —Ὅϛις ἐν τοῖς κέρδεσιν

Μίνος ἐίδοϳκι.—

Ye

Ye both are heated with intemperate warmth,
Heav'n can alone decide; let then our prayers,
United feek the fuccour of the gods.

   Tires.   What, tho' a mighty empire wait thy nod,
A monarch is but man, and I, as man,
Am not inferior to the proudeft prince.
Nor thee nor Creon, 'tis the gods I ferve,
But fince my blindnefs wakes thy infult—hear
A tale fhall fhake thy inmoft foul with horror.
Know then, a tenfold darknefs veils thy mind,
And tho' thine eyes now drink the noon-tide ray,
The time is near when they fhall quench their orbs
In everlafting night! *Blind* wretch, thou knoweft not
The long, long train of black calamities,
Whofe fcorpion ftings fhall wake thee into madnefs——
Thou know'ft not that inceftuous tranfports ftain
Thy guilty couch, and that a father's blood
Calls from the grave for vengeance : that thy plaints
Of frantic woe, fhall ring thro' ev'ry fhore,
And ev'ry mountain * a Cithæron prove.

---

  * Cithæron was the mountain on which Oedipus was expofed. There is a horrid grandeur, and local propriety in the original here, which could not well be exprefled in a tranflation. I have ventured to give it literally.

           Serene

Serene * indeed, and steady was the gale
That bore thy swelling sails to Thebes's throne;
And to Jocasta's bed: vainly thou hop'st
To anchor there in undisturb'd repose.
The port thou ridest in with such pomp of sail,
Shall wreck thee: once more give thee back
To all the madness of the hurricane ;
Thy children too—thy children did I say !
Thy breth'ren—they with curses shall repay
Thy love, when they shall find themselves allied
By guilty ties ; from the same impious stem,
Equally sprung—now let thy wanton tongue
Exhaust its rage on Creon, and on me :
I'll bear it all, but still I tell thee, prince,
The sun beholds not in its wide survey,
A wretch so guilty, so accurst as thou art.

 OED. I will not further bear thy insolence,
Be gone—haste from my presence, or by heav'n——

 TIRES. I came not here unsummon'd.

    OED. Think'st thou then,
I sent for thee, base miscreant, to insult me ?

---

* To translate this passage with spirit and delicacy was no very easy task: The passage literally runs thus—" When thou shalt have discovered that marriage, into which thou hast sail'd with a fortunate gale, where thou didst expect joy and safety, other, yes, other evils yet impend, that shall at once equal thee to thyself and thy children." The obscurity is less horrid in the original, than the translation.

TIRES.

TIRES. Thou deem'ſt me fool and mad ; far otherwiſe
-Thy parents thought.

   OED. What ſay'ſt thou ? hah ! my parents—
Whom may I call by that dear name ?

    TIRES. No more :
This day that gives thee life, ſhall prove to thee
The day of death.

   OED. What thick obſcurity   ᾽
Involves thy ev'ry ſpeech ?

    TIRES. But thou perhaps,
Who ſolv'd the Sphinx's riddle, may'ſt unfold
Their myſtery.

   OED. Doſt thou dare reproach me too
With what will ever be my greateſt triumph ?

 TIRES. That triumph ſeals thy ruin,

     OED. 'Tis well then ;
I'll glory in my fall, ſince by that fall
I've ſav'd a nation.

   TIRES. Glory then ; farewell.
Boy, lead me hence.

   OED. Aye, lead the dotard hence,
He but diſtracts our counſels.

   TIRES. Prince, I go ;

    A a 2   But,

But, ere I take of thee my laft adieu,
I will, in lefs myfterious terms, unfold
Why came *this dotard* hither. Know once more,
The man on whom thy lips have thunder'd forth
Such dreadful excerations, ftands among us.
Nor did a foreign country give him birth,
At Thebes he drew his breath; that mark thou well,
And mark—the day of vengeance is at hand.
Tho' now he riot in the fpoils of wealth,
And fhine in regal pomp, he fhall not long——.
Blindnefs, and toil, and penury are his lot,
To wafte his days in barren folitudes :
And, bending on a ftaff implore relief
From paffing travellers, who fhall fpurn him from them,
As one accurft, a blot in nature's page;
One, whom his own polluted race may call
Their father and their brother; fhe who bore him,
Her child and hufband, and his murder'd fire,
A fon inceftous, and a parricide——
Now go within thy palace, well revolve
Each word: and if one word, one circumftance
Fail, and convict me of imputed falfehood,
My art prophetic fcorn, my threats defy.

2   C H O R U S.

CHORUS.

STROPHE I.

Where lurks the murd'rous child of guilt,

By whose dark hand a monarch's blood was spilt ?

On whose devoted impious head

The Delphic rock its hallow'd curse hath shed.

Now let him mock in flight the rapid steed,

Mount * the swift storm, or seize the light'ning's speed;

For, arm'd with all the wrath of Jove,

Whose bolts of fire the redd'ning æther rend,

Apollo rushes from above,

And rav'ning destinies his steps attend.

ANTISTROPHE I.

Where steep Parnassus, wrapt in snow,

Rears 'midst incumbent heav'n his hoary brow :

Thence came the mandate of the god

To drag the monster from his drear abode :

Whether in rocks and caves, with wand'ring feet,

Like the lone † bull he seek his dark retreat,

Vain hope ! his vengeful hand to fly,

That hand which guides the stedfast universe;

To shun the light'ning of that eye

Whose searching beams its inmost center pierce.

---

* ἀιλλοποδων ἱππων; horses whose feet are like storms in swiftness.

† This idea of the solitary bull is, in the original, peculiarly forcible; Virgil likewise, with the utmost delicacy and pathos, describes the wanderings of the despairing bull—

—— —— —— Sed alter

Victus abit, longeque ignotis exulat oris.   Vide 3d Georg. 225.

STROPHE.

What founds of horror ftrike mine ear?
The awful voice of yon prophetic feer:
Tidings of death to Thebes they bring,
Denouncing vengeance to her haplefs king.
Within my breaft conflicting paffions roll,
Terror and doubt alternate fhake my foul.

How by our monarch's hand could Laïus bleed,
A ftranger to that monarch's eyes;
Uninjur'd, unprovok'd, by word or deed?
Hence let me caft the bafe furmize.

ANTISTROPHE II.

The powers who fearch the human heart,
They can alone the dreadful truth impart;
While fway'd by rage, or rival hate,
Prophets may wrongly fcan the page of fate.
Tho' high the fons of men in wifdom fhine,
Mortals can never fathom truths divine.

Could he who late the bulwark ftood,
From the fell Sphinx our city to relieve,
Defile his fpear with royal blood?
'Twere guilt to think, and madnefs to believe.

And again,
Dura jacet pernox, inftrato faxa cubili.

ACT III.

Creon, Oedipus, Jocasta, Chorus.

Creon.

THEBANS, I come to vindicate my fame
From the foul ſtains your king hath caſt upon it.
In this dark moment, or by word or deed,
If Creon aught could aggravate your woes,
He were unworthy of the air he breathes;
For what is life, if I muſt live deſpiſed
By all my countrymen, and deemed a traitor?

Chorus. 'Twas all the dictate of ungovern'd rage,
He could not think thee traitor.

       Cre. Whence could ſpring
The baſe ſuſpicion that, ſuborned by me,
The prophet utter'd lies?

     Cho. Such were his words,
But whence his thoughts aroſe I cannot ſay.

 Cre. Spoke he as if convinced?

       Cho. 'Tis not my taſk
To penetrate the hidden thoughts of kings.
Aſk him, behold he comes.

      Oed. Thou regicide!
Dar'ſt thou with all the hardineſs of guilt
Approach my palace; thou whoſe treaſonous ſchemes

             Had

Had plann'd my death, and wouldſt with rebel hand
Have torn my ſceptre from me? Tell me, traitor!
Didſt thou eſteem me fool or coward moſt,
Not to perceive thy arts, or not revenge.
This violation of the rights of princes.
I tell thee, thou art fool and madman too,
Whoſe wild ambition hurries thee away
In queſt of empire, which the peoples voice
Alone can give, and pow'rful friends ſupport.

CRE. When thou haſt heard me, then will better judge
Whether I merit this ſevere reproach.

OED. I know thy ſubtle powers of argument,
But all the force of words ſhall ne'er convince me
Thou art not ſtill my moſt inveterate foe.

CRE. Yet hear me.

OED. Talk not then of innocence.

CRE. Nay, if thou wilt not hear the voice of reaſon,
Thou groſsly err'ſt.

OED. And thou thou more groſsly ſtill,
If for this treatment of an injur'd friend
Thou hop'ſt to paſs unpuniſhed.

CRE. Prove the crime,
I will not murmur at the puniſhment.

OED. Inſidious traitor! didſt thou not adviſe
To ſummon hither this all-ſeeing prophet?

CRE.

CRE. Mine was the counfel, and in like fufpenfe
Should be repeated.

OED. Speak, what length of time
Hath Laius——

CRE. What of Laius?

OED. Thus been * flain
By hands unknown?

CRE. A long extent of years.

OED. But tell me, did Tirefias then poffefs
This power of prophecy?

CRE. Alike he fhone,
Renown'd in wifdom, and alike rever'd.

OED. Aught did he then predict concerning me.

CRE. It never reach'd my ear.

OED. What! fought ye not
The author of the murder?

CRE. Yes; but all
Prov'd fruitlefs.

OED. Why did this impoftor then,
So high renown'd, difclofe not this fell fecret?

CRE. Silence doth beft become the ignorant.
I can return no anfwer.

OED. But of this,
At leaft, thou art the judge.

CRE. Of what? O fpeak;

* The word is ᾤχετο, flow'd away; an expreffion moft forcible in the original.

B b

For

For if I can refolve thy doubts I will.

OED. Thou know'ft then, if this prophet of deceit
Had not been wrought on by thy artful wiles,
He ne'er had dar'd accufe me of this crime.

CRE. If this the feer hath done, the tafk is thine
To vindicate thyfelf: but of my crimes
I ftill am ignorant.

OED. Thy crimes? afk him.
But know—all, all thy arts fhall never prove
Thy prince a murderer!

CRE. Haft thou not efpous'd
My fifter?

OED. Yes, what then?

CRE. With pow'r fupreme
Reign you not jointly o'er the fons of Thebes?

OED. She fhares at once my kingdom and my heart;
Her will is mine: but thou——

CRE. Do I not ftand
The third in dignity?

OED. Moft undefervedly;
Thou haft betray'd thy friend.

CRE. Reftrain awhile
The tranfport of thy rage, and be convinc'd.
Where is the man, who, bleft with all that kings

And

And empires can beſtow, without their cares,

Would barter for the pageant of a name,

That peace of mind which, empires with their wealth

Can never purchaſe, or when loſt, reſtore ?

I am not mad enough to wiſh the change,

Nor hath a ſcepter ſuch alluring charms

To draw me from that purpoſe, while I ſhare

The higheſt power a ſubject can enjoy,

Or prince confer : monarchs are oft the ſlaves

Of factious nobles, oft reſign their crowns

At the mad ravings of the tyrant vulgar——

I fear them not; ſuppliant they crouch to me,

All who to fortune, or to pow'r aſpire,

And ſeek thy ſmile.   Shall I this ſolid good

Quit for a ſhadow?   No, thou wrong'ſt me much.

I ſcorn the name of traitor, and would bare

The murderous plot to light, if aught I knew

Of lurking treaſon.   Doſt thou doubt my truth,

Go learn it of the Delphic oracles;

And, if I have deceiv'd thee, let me ſuffer

All the collective wrath of heav'n and thee.

Shall prejudice uſurp the force of truth,

And ſhall a monarch, fam'd like Oedipus

For wiſdom as for virtue, doom to ſhame,

On

On blind fufpicion's moft fallacious teft,

His bofom friend? Remember, prince, the name

Of friend is facred, and, to lofe a friend,

A greater ill than lofs of life itfelf.

My innocence time only can atteft:

But wait with temper; for tho' curtain'd guilt

Is foon unveil'd, to heal the wounded fame

Of injur'd virtue afks a longer period.

 Cho. Calm thee, O king; nor let thy rage tranfport thee

Beyond the bounds of reafon: rafh refolves

Are often dearly rued.

    Oed. What! when the fword

Is lifted to my throat, muft I fubmit,

With paffive tamenefs, to the ftroke that rends

My empire from me, and, with empire, life?

 Cre. Rafh, haughty man, what will appeafe thy rage?

My exile?

  Oed. No, thy death.

    Cre. Muft I then die

Without one proof of guilt?

    Oed. Thy death, I fay,

Alone can fatisfy my juft revenge.

 Cre. Thou raveft!

    Oed. I fpeak the purpofe of my heart.

          Cre.

CRE. If so, 'tis prudent I confult my fafety.

OED. Thou traitor!

   CRE. But thou haft not prov'd me fuch.

OED. Abfolute is a king, and his commands
Muft be obey'd.

   CRE. If founded on injuftice,
They ought to be refifted unto death.

OED. Thebes, hear'ft thou this?

     CRE. Yes, hears and triumphs too.
I am her fon ; fhe taught my infant foul
The glorious precept.

   CHO. Princes, ceafe your ftrife ;
Jocafta hither from the palace bends :
Ceafe, or make her the umpire of your caufe.

Joc. Whence rofe this tumult? Thoughtlefs, cruel men,
Have you combin'd to multiply our griefs,
And plunge your country deeper in defpair?
Let each in filence to his home depart,
Nor, with your private, fwell the public woes.

CRE. Sifter, thy lord hath bafely injur'd me ;
Nought but my ruin can appeafe his rage.

OED. No, for this brother with infidious wiles
Hath plann'd my death.

   CRE. May ev'ry curfe of heav'n
Fall on me if I e'er indulg'd the thought.

        Joc.

Joc. His vows, O king, revere, and plighted faith.
If or thy country or thy queen be dear——

Cho. We too muſt join in the ſame ardent wiſh,
And plead his cauſe.

       Oed. Muſt then a baffled prince
Submit to theſe reproaches from a ſubject?

Cho. His blameleſs character, his ſolemn oath,
At leaſt demand reſpect.

       Oed. What would you have,
Or know you?

      Cho. We implore thee, prince——

             Oed. Speak on.

Cho. By friendſhip's holy name, to ſpurn not thus
One who ſo late was neareſt to thy heart,
On mere ſuſpicion.

      Oed. Then you are reſolv'd
To ſacrifice me to his dark intrigues;
For he or I muſt fall.

          Cho. By yon bright ſun,
The leader of the flaming hoſt of heav'n;
I meant not thus. 'Tis agony of ſoul
For all the woes my bleeding country bears,
Makes me thus urgent.

       Oed. Let him then be gone,

                          If

If I muſt be the victim. Not to his,

But thy requeſt I yield: deep in this heart

Will ever dwell the mem'ry of his crimes.

CRE. Unſkill'd to yield, thy ſtubborn ſoul is torn

With furied pangs; thoſe pangs are my revenge.

OED. Hence, villain, hence, leſt I revoke my words.

CRE. I go, unmov'd by all thy menaces;

That cannot ſhake my innocence, and theſe

Can beſt defend it.

CHO. Uſe thy power, O queen,

To ſoothe his mind, and urge him to retire.

Joc. But firſt inform me whence this conteſt roſe.

CHO. From vague reports, uncertain and unjuſt;

To both injurious.

Joc. What were theſe reports?

CHO. Preſs me no more, nor let us tear afreſh

The wounds of Thebes.

OED. This coldneſs in my cauſe,

Becomes you not; you ſlight the god's vice-gerent,

And yet profeſs to venerate thoſe gods.

CHO. Have I not ſworn by Phœbus, that my zeal

And duty to my prince remain unſhaken?

To love my country, and not love the man

Who ſnatch'd it from deſtruction, were to prove me

I

Bereft of reason : couldſt thou ſtretch thine arm
Once more to ſave, how would her fartheſt bounds
Ring with thy triumph !

        Joc. I conjure thee, prince,
Tell me whence ſprang this ſtrange diſſention.

                      Oed. Know,
Deareſt Jocaſta, that, with artful wiles,
Thy brother hath conſpir'd to ſeize my throne.

    Joc. Your throne, my lord ? Whence could the thought ariſe ?
    Oed. 'Twas I, he ſaid, that murder'd Laius.

                  Joc. Ha !
He could not ſpeak the dictates of his heart.

    Oed. Nay more, he hath ſuborn'd a crafty prieſt,
Who in the preſence of near half my empire,
Urg'd home the charge.

        Joc. Tho' all the race of prieſts
United to maintain the glaring lye,
Heed thou them not. No mortal eye can pierce
The dark decrees of fate : they all are bred
In ignorance, and traffic in deceit.
Thyſelf ſhall be the judge; this very prince,
Long ſince, received an oracle, the work
Of theſe ſame prieſts, (for from the god himſelf
It could not come, as ſince events have prov'd;)

                                With

With dreadful tidings that from our embrace
A fon fhould fpring, the murd'rer of his fire:
And now, we hear, that in fome gloomy fpot,
Where three ways meet, by robbers he was flain.
Yet chill'd with horror, ere the third dark morn
Rofe on our babe, we pierc'd its infant feet,
And flaves convey'd it far away from Thebes,
To perifh on the mountain's pathlefs heights.
Say then, could Phœbus utter this decree?
For neither did the fon his father flay,
Nor Laius perifh by the fate he fear'd.
Such is the boafted truth of oracles,
And let the fullen bigot hear and tremble.
Be thou convinc'd of this; that what the gods
Would have us know, they can themfelves reveal
Without the aid of thefe defigning priefts.

   OED. What fudden terrors feize me! O, my queen,
Thy words have fill'd me with amaze and horror.

   JOC. How? Wherefore?

             OED. Saidft thou not the prince was flain
Where three ways meet?

             Joc. I did; 'twas thus affirm'd,
Nor is the fact difprov'd.

             OED. But fay again,
Where, in what country did the murder happen?

        C c   Joc.

Joc. In Phocis, where the public roads divide
To Delphi and to Daulia.

OED. Mighty gods!
How long the period fince this dire event?

Joc. Not long before thy reign o'er Thebes began.
The tidings were denounced.

OED. Eternal Jove!
To what am I referv'd!

Joc. Why is thy mind
Thus agitated?

OED. Afk not, but inform me,
What were the age, form, ftature of this Laius?

Joc. In height majeftic, years had fcarcely ting'd
His locks with filver, and I've often thought
His form a faint refemblance of thy own.

OED. Diftraction!——On my own unconfcious head
I have call'd down the curfe of every god!

Joc. O heavens, I fhudder as I gaze upon thee——

OED. Too well, I fear, the prophet knew my fate!
One farther circumftance will prove my guilt,
Or feal my innocence.

Joc. Tho' my lips faulter,
Yet afk, and if I know, I will reveal it.

OED. Went he attended with a chofen few,
Or with the pomp and fplendor of a monarch?

Joc.

Joc. His train confifted but of five; of thefe
One was the herald; and one only chariot
That carried Laius.

Oed. Then my guilt is fure,
Glaring as yonder fun: but who brought back
The tidings of his death? .

Joc. One who alone
Efcap'd the gen'ral flaughter.

Oed. Lives he now
Within this palace?

Joc. No; his lord no more,
When he beheld thee on the throne of Thebes,
With earneft fupplication at my feet,
He fought permiffion to depart from Thebes,
To feed my diftant flocks, nor I refus'd,
For he was ever the moft faithful fervant.

Oed. O hafte, let him be fummon'd inftantly.

Joc. He fhall; but why thus eagerly defire
This ftranger's coming?

Oed. I am on the rack: '
'His anfwers may refolve my doubts, and oh!
May plunge me in defpair; yet my refolve
Is fix'd to fee him.

Joc. He will foon be here.

But

But oh! my lord, permit thy faithful queen
To fearch the bottom of this fecret wound
That rankles at thy heart.

    OED. Thou fhalt know all:
Since thy own fate is clofely link'd with mine,
To thee I will unbofom all my foul.
My father, Polybus, enjoys the throne
Of Corinth; Merope, his royal fpoufe,
By birth a Dorian; there I long poffefs'd
Riches and pow'r next only to fupreme,
Till one event, moft trivial in itfelf,
But dreadful in its iffue, crufh'd my joys.
A drunken courtier 'midft his cups proclaim'd
That Polybus was not my rightful fire.
Kindling at this, I fcarce contain'd my rage
Till of my parents I enquir'd the truth
Of this bafe faying; they alike incens'd,
Threaten'd with death the author of the charge.
This calm'd my prefent fears, but ftill my mind
Labour'd with fecret doubts. Refolv'd to fearch
This myftery of my birth, by private roads
I fought the Pythian fhrine; the holy maid
Nought of my birth or parentage reveal'd;
But thus, convuls'd with raving extafies,

              Read

Read the dark page of fate—" Thou, wretch, art doom'd
" To ftain thy mother's bed, from thence to raife
" A race accurft, and laft with impious hand
" To flay the hoary fire who gave thee birth."
Shudd'ring with horror at thefe awful founds,
With hafty ftep, from Corinth's fatal towers
I urg'd my way. Directed by the ftars,
O'er tracklefs waftes and folitary lands,
To that lone fpot where haplefs Laius fell:
Ah fhake not thus, for I will tell thee all—
Juft as I reach'd the pafs, where three ways meet,
A chariot met my fight, where foremoft fat,
Who feem'd a herald; but within reclin'd
Another, and appear'd of regal port,
In age, and form, and every circumftance
Refembling moft the man thy words defcribe.
Both rufh'd againft me, and with fury ftrove
To drive me back; refentment fir'd my foul:
Inftant I fell'd the charioteer to earth,
And fprang to meet the chariot, where the fage
Obfervant fate, and twice with all his might
Smote me upon the temples; but in death
Soon wail'd the rafh affault: befmear'd with gore,
Beneath my ftaff he fell, and bit the ground.

His·

His fervants in the general conteft fell;

Not one, I thought, efcap'd to tell the news.

If this were Laius—who, thro' earth's wide bound,

Is half fo wretched as myfelf, or who

Like me accurft ?   No friendly citizen

Muft fuccour my diftrefs, or ftranger ope

The hofpitable door, but drive me hence,

Far hence, in defart folitudes to weep,

And 'midft the favage wandr'ers feek a home.

But oh my bittereft pang, thefe lips pronounc'd

The dire decree that drives me from the land,

From Thebes, from thee, and all my foul holds dear,

A foul, inceftuous, bloody parracide !

Ah whither fhall I go; to Corinth?   There

I feek inceftuous tranfports, there I flay

The beft of friends and fathers.   Sure fome fiend

Hurries me on thro' all this maze of guilt.

But O! ye mightier powers, who rule on high,

Ere fuch a fcene of horror overwhelm me,

Crufh this devoted head, and let me find

In death a refpite from feverer toils.

   Cho.   O King, we more than fhare in all thy griefs;

Perhaps the fhepherd may difperfe your fears ;

Defpair not.

      Oed.   All my hopes are center'd there.

Joc.

Joc.   What is he to reveal?

                    Oed.   If he confirm
The thing thou fay'ft, then am I free from guilt.

   Joc.   What have I faid?

                    Oed.   Thou faid'ft the king was flain
By robbers on his journey; if he fell
By numbers, I am fafe : my fingle arm
The ftranger flew; but if by one alone,
I am that wretch.

                    Joc.   Doubt not his firft report,
From which he dares not fwerve.   Not only I,
The whole affembled city heard the tale.
But if he fwerve, it ftill remains to prove
That oracles themfelves are not impoftures;
For tho' their vaunted god had fix'd his death
On my poor murder'd child, that child thou feeft
Perifh'd long fince on bleak Cithæron's top.
Henceforth my foul is fteel'd againft belief
Of priefts and prophecies.

                    Oed.   And well it may;
But inftantly difpatch fome trufty flave
To bring this fhepherd.

                    Joc.   Thou fhalt be obey'd
This inftant; let us go within the palace.
My pride is to obey thee; and my joy
Is then the greateft when I pleafe thee moft.

C H O R U S.
STROPHE I.

Eternal Jove! my heart infpire
With ardent virtue's active zeal, to hear
Thy voice obedient, and thy laws revere;

 Thofe heav'n-defcended laws, almighty fire,
Which thy creative energy impreft
On animated nature's infant breaft.

 Daughters of light, unlike the race of earth,
Who range the tracts of day with * fteps fublime;

 Still vigorous like the god who gave you birth,
Beyond the grafp of fate, or bound of time.

ANTISTROPHE I.

'Twas infolence firft drench'd in blood
The tyrant's hand; but when elate with pride
He fpurns at right, and dares the gods deride.

 From the proud precipice where late he ftood,
That infolence fhall dafh him headlong down,
To wail his cruelty and ravifh'd crown.

 To thee, dread ruler of events below,
In deep humility behold we bend,

 Wifdom and life from thee their fountain flow;
Oh! from yon heav'ns thy inftant fuccour fend.

---

* Υψίποδις γάζωιαν ὁ αιθέζα τεκνωβότης—

STROPHE

STROPHE II.

Where do the deſtin'd ſons of rapine rove,
Who ſlight the awful voice of nature's God,
Nor bend with rev'rence at his high abode.

    The thunder ſtruggling in the graſp of Jove.
With ſtrong vibration labours to be gone,
And ſweep them to the gulph of Acheron.

    If vice triumphant rear her purple creſt,
And injur'd virtue lift her voice in vain,
    Still ſhall the tyrant fiend uſurp the breaſt,
And vainly do we raiſe the choral ſtrain.

ANTISTROPHE II.

Flaming with holy zeal no more
To Delphi ſhall the prieſts of Jove repair,
Or where Olympia's turrets riſe in air,

    With gifts and ſongs the gods implore;
If impious tongues thoſe rites prophane,
And treat their mandates with diſdain:

    Lord of the univerſe! their pride controul,
Avenge thine own; aſſert Apollo's cauſe;

    And flaſh conviction on the ſtubborn ſoul
That ſpurns thy precepts, and reſiſts thy laws.

D d

A C T IV.

<small>MESSENGER, CHORUS, JOCASTA, OEDIPUS, SHEPHERD.</small>

MESSENGER.

SAGES and chiefs of Thebes, 'tis my refolve,
With incenfe, and with fuppliant boughs, to feek
The temple of the gods : your prince, fo high
For wifdom fam'd, and fortitude of foul,
Forgets that he is man.   His mind is torn
With difmal terrors of he knows not what,
And fhrinks at each unmeaning tale he hears :
I urge, intreat, expoftulate in vain—
Heav'n is provok'd, I fear; on thee we call,
All-feeing Phœbus, neareft ftill to hear
The wretch's plaint, arm thou his wav'ring thought
With wonted firmnefs.   He whofe fkilful hand
Should guide our bark, the pilot of the ftate,
Sinks at the helm, and the tumultuous fea
Will foon ingulph us all.

   MESSEN.   Inform me, ftrangers,
Where fhall I find the palace of your king,
Or fooneft where himfelf?

    CHO.   This is his palace:

The

The king is now within; thou feeft his queen.

Mess. Is fhe indeed the wife of Oedipus?
Moft happy may fhe live, nor fhe alone,
But all around her fhare the gen'ral joy.

Joc. I thank thee, ftranger, for thy friendly greeting;
But quickly tell me wherefore art thou come,
And what thy tidings?

Mess. Welcome, mighty princefs,
To thee and Oedipus.

Joc. What are they, fay;
And whence thyfelf?

Mess. From Corinth, and I bring
News that will give you both delight and grief.

Joc. Inftant explain thy meaning.

Mess. If report
Lye not, the race of Ifthmus have refolv'd
That Oedipus fhall reign o'er Corinth.

Joc. How?
Is not then Polybus their king?

Mess. He was;
But death hath laid the hoary king in duft.

Joc. How! Polybus no more?

Mess. May more than death
Befall thy flave, if his report prove falfe.

Joc. Hafte to thy mafter with the joyful news.

Fly

Fly inftant;—where, ye lying oracles,
Diviners, where is now your boafted truth,.
Prophets and Priefts? For Oedipus long fince,
Fearing left he fhould fhed this monarch's blood,
As Phœbus had foretold, from Corinth fled
In willing exile. Now forfooth we hear
That by the common courfe of fate he died,
Without or fraud, or violence.

     OED. O! my queen,
Why am I fummon'd from my palace hither?

 JOC. For this; to learn the truth of oracles:
That ftranger there will beft explain my words.

  OED. Who is he? Whence, and what his meffage, fay.

 JOC. He comes from Corinth, and his tidings are,
That Polybus, your father, is no more.

  OED. Is this thy meffage; is it thus indeed?

  MESS. Ev'n as the queen hath faid.

      OED. But fpeak again:
How died the prince; by treafon or difeafe?

  MESS. Ah prince, a little violence will bow
The languid limbs of age.

    OED. Difeafe then crufh'd
The good old monarch.

    MESS. Yes, difeafe in part,

          And

And part the preſſure of a length of years,

For he had * meaſur'd out the life of man.

    Oed. 'Tis well : what blinded wretch will now regard

Altars, and prieſts, and birds of ominous wing,

Screaming aloft ? whoſe falſe and baſe decrees

Had plung'd my hand in blood, a father's blood,

Who died, it ſeems, remote from Thebes and me,

Bow'd down with weight of years : theſe hands unſtain'd,

And guiltleſs of his blood. Unleſs, perchance,

Continual ſorrow for the loſs of me

Prey'd on his heart, and hurried on his fate.

Thus only could I cauſe his death : but he

Sleeps in the boſom of the grave ; nor prieſts,

Nor oracles ſhall break his long repoſe.

    Joc. Did I not tell thee this ?

                    Oed. Thou didſt ; but ſtill

Severeſt apprehenſions ſhook my ſoul.

    Joc. Away with them for ever.

                    Oed. But the bed

Of inceſt, how it harrows up my thoughts !

---

* Μακρῶ γε συμμιτ꜕ημαϛ κϛεω.

  The ſame expreſſion occurs in the Pſalms ;

  " Make me to know the meaſure of my days,"

                        39th Pſalm, 4th Verſe.

                                Joc.

Joc. Let not vain terrors agitate thy mind;
Man is the fport of chance; the pow'rs divine
Loft in the nobler pleafures of the fkies,
Need not our reptile race.   The tafk be his
To hufband well his life, and rove at large
Where fancy leads, or pleafure points the way.
Fear not th' inceftuous bed, nor be the flave
Of frantic zeal nor fuperftitious dreams:
For oft, amidft the flumbers of the night,
Have men in vifions reap'd inceftuous joys.
True happinefs is his, who boldly fpurns
Such vain chimeras.

        Oed.   True; but ftill fhe lives,
This mother, whom I dread, and I muft fly
Th' accurft embrace.

        Joc.   Go to thy father's grave;
Let that inform thee what thou haft to fear.

  Oed.   Yet, yet I fhudder: and, while fhe furvives,
I ftill muft tremble.

        Mess.   Say, illuftrious prince,
What is this woman whom thou fear'ft fo much?

  Oed.   'Tis Merope, my friend, the late efpous'd
Of Polybus.

    Mess.   But whence proceed your fears?

                              Oed.

OED. From oracles moft dreadful to relate!

MESS. And may a ftranger know them?

OED. Thou fhalt hear:

Apollo hath denounc'd, that I fhould ftain

A mother's bed with inceft, and thefe hands

Drench in paternal blood—For this, long fince,

I fled from Corinth, and have here enjoy'd

Each earthly blifs, fave that moft fweet of all,

The dear delight a parent's prefence gives.

MESS. Was this the motive of thy exile?

OED. This,

This dread alone of parricidal guilt——

MESS. What if I prove the meffenger of joy,

And bring thee tidings fuch as may difperfe

Thy every doubt?

OED. Ah, deareft ftranger, fpeak them;

Thy recompence fhall be moft princely.

MESS. Yes,

I come to chafe thy fears, relieve thy doubts,

And hail thee back to Corinth.

OED. Never, never!

While one of thofe dear parents ftill furvives,

Will I return to Corinth!

MESS. Son, I fee

Thy

Thy ignorance hath caused these idle fears.

OED. Indeed! By heav'n inform me where I err.

MESS, If for this cause thou fled'st.

      OED. The curse denounc'd
By Phœbus, drove me into willing exile.

MESS, The dread of murder, and inceſtuous crimes.

OED. The ſame.

   MESS. Thy fears are groundleſs.

      OED. Not if theſe
My parents were, or true the voice of Jove.

MESS. Know then that Polybus by ties of blood
Was never bound to thee.

   OED. How? Speak again :
Not Polybus my ſire!

   MESS. No more than mine.

OED. And yet he call'd me ſon.

    MESS. His by adoption.
Theſe hands firſt gave thee to his fond embrace.

OED. And could an alien kindle in his ſoul
A father's tranſports?

   MESS. He had never known
A father's joys.

  OED. Was I by purchaſe thine,
Or may I hail thee by a father's name?

          MESS.

Mess. I found thee in a deep and darkfome ˌ ˈˈ
Of Mount Cithæron.

        Oed. Ha! what led thee there?

Mess. My flocks, that ranged the mountains verdant fides.

Oed. Thou wert a fhepherd then it feems.

               Mess. I was;
And more, the fhepherd that preferv'd thy life.

Oed. What had befall'n me, ere thy guardian hand
Snatch'd me from death?

        Mess. The joints of thy own feet
Will beft inform thee what.

          Oed. Ah why repeat
That antient malady?

        Mess. Mine was the hand
That loofed their tendons from the intangling cords.

Oed. Thus early did my woes commence?

             Mess. To this
Thou oweft the name of Oedipus.

          Oed. Ah me!
Which of my parents could be thus inhuman;
Canft thou inform me?

        Mess. That he beft can tell
Who gave thee to me.

         Oed. Then thou found'ft me not;

             E e   But

But from another didſt receive me?

      MESS. Yes,

A brother ſhepherd gave thee to my charge.

 OED. O ſpeak his name, his reſidence, whate'er
Thou know'ſt of this ſame ſhepherd.

       MESS. He was call'd
A ſervant of king Laius.

     OED. Laius? ha!
The ſame who govern'd Thebes?

      MESS. The very ſame:
He was his ſhepherd.

    OED. Is he ſtill alive;
Could I behold him?

    MESS. Theſe his countrymen
Can better tell thee.

    OED. O my friends, declare
If aught ye know, or aught, perchance, have heard
Of ſuch a ſhepherd; whether he reſides
At Thebes, or in the country; inſtant ſpeak:
'Tis of the laſt importance to our welfare.

 CHO. O king, if right we judge, he ſeems the man
Whom thou haſt lately ſummon'd: but the Queen
Is beſt acquainted.

   OED. Princeſs, doſt thou know

              Whether

Whether the man this shepherd hath describ'd,
And he whom thou hast sent for, be the same?

Joc. I know not what he said, or whom he meant:
Nor is there aught of moment in his words;
Dark, idle words; thou art too anxious, prince:
Act not thus rashly.

        Oed. What? Must I neglect
To trace this mystery of my birth, when now
The path is open, and the prospect fair?

Joc. By heav'n forbear; I tell thee 'tis a rock
Thy peace will split on: if thou valuest life
Or happiness, forbear. O this torn heart!

Oed. Hence, woman, with thy fears; I am resolv'd:
Were all my ancestors a race of slaves,
'Twere no disgrace to thee; I sav'd your empire;
In that one deed was more nobility,
Than all the glories of your line can boast.

Joc. By all thy soul holds dear, beware the search.

Oed. Not all thy eloquence can shake my purpose·
To trace this matter to the very source.

Joc. Oh hear my better counsel, and forbear:
Shun it as death.

        Oed. Thy counsel but involves me·

In tenfold error.

       Joc.   Wretched, wretched prince!
May heav'n still hide the secret from thy view,
Nor curse thee with the knowledge of thy birth.

    Oed.   Let other messengers be sent, in haste,
To bring this lingering shepherd to our presence:
And leave the queen to glory in her birth,
And antient lineage.

       Joc.   Wretched, wretched prince;
Obstinate, headlong, to thy own destruction
I leave thee to a search which thou shalt rue
For ever—treasure in thy heart those words;
Remember they're my last—my last! farewell.

                     [*Exit* Jocasta.

    Cho.   Sire, didst thou mark Jocasta's fix'd despair!
With what confused and eager looks she fled:
Much, much I fear her silence does presage
Events of dreadful issue!

    Oed.   Let them come:
Still my resolve is fix'd to penetrate
This mighty cloud that hangs around my birth:
Whate'er my fate, I must not, will not more
Be kept in darkness: this it is that stings
Her haughty soul: she thinks that I shall prove

Of

Of rank, and parents, humbler than her own.
Blind woman! but my parents were not mean.
Thou wert my mother, fortune; and thy fon
Glories in his defcent: fublimer far
Than all the kings of earth: the kindred months,
Offspring of time, coeval with the world,
Salute me as they roll their mighty round,
And call me brother.   Led thro' arduous toils,
By you I triumph on the throne of Thebes,
Power in my nod, and fortune in my fmile:
And from the glorious height look down fecure,
Whoe'er my fire, a monarch or a flave.

STROPHE.

A prophet's fpirit warms my foul!
I fee, I fee the mighty vifions dawn;
    And all the fcenes of fate unroll!
By great Olympus, ere another morn,
Cithæron, fkirt thy dufky front with gold,
Thou fhalt the long, myfterious maze unfold.
    Then to our king fhall fwell the choral fong,
Our feet in myftic dance more fwiftly move;
    And while our grateful meafures we prolong,
Phœbus fhall liften, and the ftrain approve.

A N-

ANTISTROPHE.

What bright celestial gave thee birth ?
O thou, whose wisdom speaks that birth divine:
Renown'd above the sons of earth ;
From Jove descended, or the sister Nine.
Say art thou sprung from sylvan Pan's embrace,
With some fair daughter of ætherial race ;
Or wert thou nourish'd in Cyllene's groves,

Where Mercury the swifter nymphs pursues ;
Or on the sacred hills where Bacchus roves,

And courts in laurel bow'rs the bashful muse ?

OED. Friends, if my judgment err not, yonder sage,
This way advancing, is the same whom late
We summon'd hither; both in age, and mien,
Resembling whom this stranger hath describ'd.
My servants too support him : you, perchance,
May better know him.

CHO. 'Tis the same, my lord,
The faithful shepherd of our good old king.

OED. Stranger, is this the man ?

MESS. I know him well.

OED. Old man, draw near ; look up with confidence,
And answer faithfully what I shall ask.

Didst

Didſt thou not live with Laius?

     SHEP. Yes, my lord;

Nor was I of the hireling train, but bred

Within this palace.

    OED. What thy office, ſpeak?

 SHEP. My office was to tend the royal ſheep.

 OED. And whither chiefly didſt thou lead thoſe ſheep?

 SHEP. To Mount Cithæron, and the neighbouring plains.

 OED. Say, doſt thou recollect that ſtranger's face?

 SHEP. That ſtranger—who? Whence is he? What his crime?

 OED. I ſay again, reflect; and call to mind

If thou haſt ever had, or intercourſe,

Or converſe with him.

    SHEP. Sire, with age, and cares,

My memory fails.

    MESS. Nor is there cauſe of wonder:

But I'll refreſh his memory, and recount

Some antient facts he ſoon will call to mind.

I am that ſhepherd who for three whole months,

Thro' long ſucceſſive years, thy friendſhip ſhar'd

On Mount Cithæron's heights—early as ſpring

Bade the young herbage ſhoot; ev'n till the riſe

Of pale Arcturus: and when winter's froſts

Deform'd the year, each with his ſev'ral fiocks

          Departed

Departed homeward; to my cottage I,

And thou to Laius' palace: have thefe fcenes

Entirely fled thy thoughts?

                  SHEP. Almoft they had;

For 'tis a long, long period fince.

                  MESS. 'Tis true:

But can'ft thou, fhepherd, to remembrance call

An infant whom I once receiv'd from thee,

And promis'd all a father's foftering care?

    SHEP. An infant, friend? What means thy queftion?

                        MESS. This,

This is that infant, whom thou now behold'ft.

    SHEP. Away with thee, thou rav'ft: perdition feize

Thy traitor's tongue.

              OED. Why art thou thus incens'd?

Thou art thyfelf more worthy of reproof.

    SHEP. In what have I offended?

                OED. By thy rage,

And filence touching this fame child.

              SHEP. Ah, Sir,

He knew not what he faid.

            OED. Eafe my fufpenfe,

Or by the gods I'll force the fecret from thee.

                                SHEP.

SHEP. Ah ven'rate hoary age!

        OED. Quick, bind his hands.

SHEP. What muſt I do, my lord, or what diſcloſe?

OED. Delay not, but inform me, didſt thou give
An infant to this man?

        SHEP. I did, and oh!
Death had that moment been my happieſt boon.

OED. This day thou dieſt, unleſs I know the whole
Of this dark ſcene.

        SHEP. Ah ſpare the dire recital:
'Tis death to tell thee.

        OED. Doſt thou trifle with me?

SHEP. Did I not ſay I gave the child?

        OED. Go on;
Whence came he? Was he thine by birth, or who
Conſign'd him to thy charge?

        SHEP. He was not mine;
I had receiv'd him from another hand.

OED. What other? Speak his name, and where he dwells.

SHEP. By all the pow'rs above, enquire no more:
I do conjure thee.

        OED. If I aſk again,
Wretch, thou ſhalt die.

        SHEP. In yonder palace born——

        F f   OED.

OED. Sprung from a flave, or was the king his fire?

SHEP. Oh mifery to declare—

        OED. Oh! Death to hear!

Yet fpeak——

      SHEP. He was fuppos'd the king's own fon.

But well Jocafta knows the gloomy truth;

She can inftruct thee beft.

         OED. Didft thou from her

Receive the child?

        SHEP. 'Twere fruitlefs to deny

What fate itfelf reveals.

        OED. What was her purpofe?

SHEP. That I fhould kill it.

         OED. What, deftroy the child?

Bloody, inhuman parent!

       SHEP. Dire affright,

From dreadful oracles, compell'd the queen

. To this unnatural deed.

      OED. How, oracles?

What did they threaten?

       SHEP. That this fon fhould flay

Thofe who begat him.

      OED. But if fuch her fears,

Why didft thou give it to this fhepherd's care?

3

SHEP. Compaffion for the infant wrung my foul;
I hop'd he would have borne his charge away,
Far, far from Thebes, and thefe his native roofs :
Fatal miftake! that life to him was death,
Preferv'd to long, unutterable woes——
For oh! if thou be'ft he, thou art indeed
The moft ill-fated, moft accurft of men.

OED. 'Tis done; the tenfold myftery burfts to light;
I am that moft ill-fated, moft accurft.
Thou fun farewell; why fmile thy beams on me,
Whom murder blackens, and whom inceft ftains?
Inceft and murder of the deepeft hue:
A father flain, a mother's bed defil'd!
Come night, come horror fhield me from his rays;
Plunge me in thick impenetrable glooms,
Black as my crimes, and boundlefs as my guilt.

C H O R U S.

O man, thou fhadow of a fhade!
How foon thy brighteft glories fade!
What higher boon could fortune give,
What nobler gifts could man receive,
Than late fhe fhower'd on our devoted king;
Only to plunge him deeper in defpair,
And ratify the folemn truths we fing?

At

At yon sad spectacle of woe,

Who can refrain the starting tear!

What tongue the bitter plaint forbear,

" That mis'ry is the lot of all below!"

Blind fav'rite of a nymph more blind,

She bade thee dart thy rapid flight

Beyond the bound to mortal pride assign'd;

And plac'd thee on her dizziest height:

Then thine arm the monster slew,

Dreadful with her forked fang,

Whose eagle pinions mock'd the wind,

And ravening, as in quest of blood she flew,

To Thebes the prophecies of death she sang——

For this, thy hand the scepter shar'd,

An empire was thy great reward.

But now what sounds of horror meet mine ear?

How art thou blasted in thy bright career!

How chang'd in one dark, fatal hour,

Dash'd from the soaring pinnacle of pow'r,

And all that mortals vaunt of high and great,

To wrestle with the toils of fate.

Thrice wretched prince, renown'd in vain,

Since all the trophies of thy fame

Throw but a guilty splendour round thy woes;

Unchill'd

Unchill'd with horror, who thofe crimes fhall name
Whofe dark, indelible, eternal ftain,
With infamy pollutes thy bed,
And dooms to vengeance thy devoted head.
How could thy confcious bed fo long fuftain
Its guilty load, thro' night's incumbent gloom,
Nor ftart with horror, and a voice affume!
But fate hath bared the deed to light,
Hath bar'd to our aftonifh'd fight
A father murder'd by his child,
A mother by that fon's embrace defil'd.
O that thefe eyes might ne'er behold thee more,
But diftant far their duteous forrows pour :
By thee we rais'd them up to life and light,
Only to plunge them in eternal night.

ACT

ACT V.

CHORUS, MESSENGER, OEDIPUS, CREON.

Enter another MESSENGER.

MESSENGER.

MOST honour'd chiefs of this once happy land,
Rouze all the refolution man can boaft
To fortify your fouls, while I relate
A direr tale than ever reach'd your ears—
Unfold a fcene to your aftonifh'd eyes
More black with woe than e'er thofe eyes beheld:
Not the broad Danube's waves, nor Phafis ftream,
Can purge away the complicated crimes
That ftain thefe guilty roofs; in dark array
They rife to view, and as they rife, pollute
The fickening light—fate rules the gloomy hour,
And rafh defpair, impatient, rufhes on
To deeds of added horror.

     CHO. Added horror!

We

We thought the catalogue of this day's woes
Already fwell'd beyond the pow'r of fate.

   MESS. No; to compleat our fufferings, fhe referves
A ftroke more dreadful ftill : the queen is flain.

   CHO. Jocafta flain—by whom? What daring hand——

   MESS. She dar'd herfelf the deed : no confcious eye
Was witnefs to her death. What we beheld
Thefe faultering lips fhall tell. With hafty ftep,
Enrag'd, fhe burft within the palace gates——
Then, rufhing to the bridal chamber, tore,
With favage fury, her diforder'd hair;
Invoking Laius from the tomb to view
A wretch, the fatal fource of all his woes,
Who bore his murderer, clafp'd the parricide,
That fon, that murd'rer, in abhorr'd embrace,
And ftain'd his bed with inceft; then with fhrieks
Of wildeft grief, fhe wail'd th' accurfed couch
That witnefs'd to her dark, forbidden joys :
Nor heard we more; for inftant we beheld
The wretched Oedipus, in frantic mood,
Raving thro' all the dome : with thund'ring voice
Commanding us to bring him fword or fpear,
To end his hated being. " Lead me where
Thefe eyes, e'er veil'd in darknefs, may behold

That

'That injur'd form I dare not call my wife ;
Her who begat me, her, whofe glowing limbs,
Unconfcious, clafp'd the hufband and the child."
Inftant, by fome infpiring dæmon led,
He rufh'd upon the double doors that clos'd
The unhappy queen, and from their brazen bolts
Tore them, while far and wide the hollow dome
Refounded back his cries : but foon new fcenes
Of horror met our fight, the royal fair
All pale and breathlefs, in the fatal noofe
Entangled.   Shuddering at the view, the prince
Recoil'd : then loofing the fufpended cord,
Heav'd a deep groan, and flung him on the ground,
Convuls'd awhile with agonies of grief.
When fudden ftarting, from her robe he tore
The golden buckle that adorn'd her fide,
And madly plung'd the points into his eyes,
Exclaiming, " Never more fhall I behold
Or thee, unhappy woman, or the race
Sprung from thy loins." Bellowing thefe horrid plaints,
He pierc'd, he tore from out their mangled orbs,
The balls of fight : inftant the gufhing blood
Its fluices burft, and, rufhing down his cheeks,
Pour'd the black flood that ftain'd his princely form.

Such

Such are the complicated ills that crufh'd

This wretched pair.   Who lately * reign'd fupreme

In mutual blifs, are now fupreme alone

In mifery : curft with more than common woes !

Their joy was boundlefs ; boundlefs was the guilt

Of fuch an union ; boundlefs are their fufferings.

Ah ! how hath one black fatal morn o'ercaft

The cloudlefs fcene! how blafted all their joys!

On ev'ry fide are heard the mingled founds

Of groans, defpair and death——the difmal cries

Of murderer and of inceft——all the ftores

Of fecret anguifh, and fevere diftrefs,

At once difcharging their collective rage.

    Cho.   Where is the haplefs prince?

              Mess.   Throw wide, he cries,

Throw wide the gates, and let all Thebes behold

The murderer of his fire, with inceft black,

With blood defil'd, and crimes without a name——

Lead me, O lead me from thefe guilty roofs,

To banifhment, to death——that banifhment

My lips denounc'd will be my beft relief

* Great emphafis is in the original laid on the comparifon of the prefent with the former
ftate of Oedipus; which the Tranflator could not well convey to the reader without a pa-
raphrafe of the two or three fucceeding lines.

From all th' infufferable ills that rufh,

With overwhelming rage, at once upon me.

But words are weak: behold a fcene that fpeaks

Beyond the boldeft pow'rs of eloquence;

A fcene fo full of horror, it would move

His moft inveterate foe.

    CHO. Ah! fight of grief

Beyond whate'er my darkeft fears had fram'd.

Rafh man! what furious dæmon urg'd thee on

To this dire act; thus to accumulate

Woe upon woe to crufh thy haplefs head?

Moft wretched of the wretched! my fwoll'n heart

Had much to utter; but muft burft itfelf

In filence, for the fight of fuch diftrefs

Hath ftruck me dumb for ever.

    Enter OEDIPUS.

    OED. Hah! where am I?

What plaintive accents vibrate on my ear,

That feem to pity one whom fate hath plac'd

Beyond the pow'r of pity to relieve!—

Fortune, my mother, whither art thou fled?

 CHO. She hath forfaken thee; hath plung'd thee down

In an abyfs of woes.

    OED. O dark! dark! dark!

Dark without dawn of hope, or beam of day!

          I ftand

I ſtand envelop'd in eternal ſhade :
Remembrance like a fury ſtings my ſoul,
While my own paſſions ſharpen ev'ry goad,
And drive me on to madneſs.

     Cho. Doubly curſt
Both in a huſband's and a father's hopes,
Well may thy reaſon fail thee in this hour
Of multifold affliction.

    Oed. Art thou here!
Thou, once my friend and guide in happier hours,
This, this was Oedipus.——Abject and blind,
Thou wilt not leave me to ſeverer pangs.

 Cho. What haſt thou done ? What vengeful god impell'd
To this mad deed ?

    Oed. Phœbus himſelf,—yes, Phœbus,
Is that avenging, that impulſive pow'r.
That I am blind, impute to me alone,
'Twas I who quench'd thoſe orbs, whoſe light but ſerv'd
To kindle horror, and awake deſpair.

 Cho. Ah! dreadful truth !

    Oed. What, what remains
Grateful to me, in voice, or ſight, or ſound ?
Each joy extinct, and earth one barren void.
Rouze you, my friends, in injur'd virtue's cauſe ;

          Drive

Drive from your land this peſtilential bane,

This monſter, black with inceſt and with blood;

This moſt abhorr'd of gods, and all mankind.

    Cho.   Thy ſuff'rings make thee rave. Ah! fatal hour

When firſt I hail'd thee on the throne of Thebes!

    Oed.   And Oh! more fatal hour that ſaw my feet

Loos'd from their bands on bleak Cithæron's height.

Curſt be the hand that loos'd them. 'Twas not life

That hand beſtow'd; 'twas death. I then had died

In innocence, nor known, nor caus'd a pang.

    Cho. Oh thus had fate ordain'd——

                            Oed. I had not then

Imbrued my hand in blood—I had not then

Receiv'd Jocaſta to my guilty bed.

I ſhould not then—

              Cho. How! What ſhall I advife thee,

Since death itſelf were better far than life

Waſted in mis'ry and perpetual gloom?

    Oed.   The loſs of ſight, my friends, I leaſt bewail:

Ah! with what * eyes in Pluto's dark domain,

---

   * It appears from this paſſage, that the antients ſuppofed the fame qualities both of mind
and body to be poſſeſſed by the dead which they had while living.

   Thus Virgil: —— Laniatum corpore toto

           Deiphobum videt, et lacerum crudeliter ora.

                       Æneid. lib. 6. 495.

                                Could

Could Oedipus have view'd his murder'd fire,
Cover'd with wounds, and welt'ring in the blood
His impious offspring fpilt; or her who bore
The parricidal wretch, whofe foul embrace
Hath ftain'd the confcious womb that gave him life?
Could e'er this heart a parent's joy have known,
To view the offspring of that foul embrace,
Tho' fair in virgin beauty, haft'ning on
Thro' long progreffive mifery, to complete
The meafure of my woes, and fhare my guilt!
Ah! never, never could thefe eyes behold them;
Never the lofty citadels of Thebes,
Her gilded palaces, her beauteous fanes,
And her bold race that own'd me king in vain,
Since now debas'd below the meaneft flave.
Oh painful, bitter change! Thefe lips pronounc'd
The curft decree that drives me from the land
The execrated fcorn of you and heav'n,
A foul, inceftuous, bloody parricide.——
Thus with a thoufand objects compafs'd round,
To wound anew my agonizing heart,
Blindnefs is but relief from weightier ills.
Grant me, ye mighty rulers of the world,
Some pow'r to bar the paffages of found,

To

To shut each sense, and quite extinguish thought;
For ev'ry sense is now alive to woe.
Ah why, Cithæron, did thy arched glooms
Lend their broad shade to screen my infant head?
Why did not some devouring savage rend
My scatter'd limbs, and give them to the winds;
That my disgraceful birth might never stain
The annals of mankind?—O Polybus,
And thou, O Corinth, falsely deem'd my country,
How have ye nourish'd in these princely robes,
Beneath this specious form a canker'd wound,
Putrid and rank! for now I stand confess'd
Base in myself, and base in my descent.
Ye conscious forests, ye wide-spreading glades,
And thou dark avenue, where three ways meet,
That drank the blood of my expiring sire;
Witness what guilty transports fill'd my breast
When I beheld his hoary figure fall
Prostrate and bite the ground—how am I chang'd!
How dearly have I rued the triumph, bought
At the high price of ev'ry other joy:
Flung headlong from the bliss of gods, to wail
With dæmons in the hell of deep despair!
O fatal, fatal nuptials! Night of horror!

How

How have ye ſtamp'd pollution on the names
Of father, brother, ſon—how burſt the band
Of dear relation! Sure around the bed
Some fierce preſiding dæmon fix'd his ſtand,
And ſow'd the ſeeds of ev'ry baneful ill.
Reflection ſhudders at the black detail——
I cannot bear the retroſpect: my tongue
Faulters with ſhame, and ev'ry ſinew ſhrinks.
Wherefore, by all the gods, approach, and ſlay
This victim to my own and others crimes.
Or bear me to ſome bleak and barren iſle,
Where ſound of human voice was never heard;
Or plunge me in the deep with all my crimes.
Fear not, my friends, approach; black as I am,
Ye cannot, by the touch, partake the guilt,
Whoſe weight ſhall cruſh this guilty head alone.

Cho. Moſt opportunely Creon this way bends;
Creon, on whom thy pow'r and kingly ſway
Will ſoon devolve, as next of royal line:
His counſel beſt will guide us thro' this maze
Of intricate ſuſpenſe.

Oed. What ſay'ſt thou,—Creon?
That Creon, whom I late ſo baſely injur'd,
What can I ſay to him; or how find words
At once expreſſive of my ſhame and grief!

CRE

We learn to venerate that pow'r whose laws
Thou haft thus violated, thus prophan'd.

Oed.   But one word more, and I have done for ever—
By every bond of friendſhip I conjure thee,
By all the ties of nature, to decree
Sepulchral honours worthy of her birth,
And each due rite the illuſtrious dead demand,
To thy dear ſiſter, and my hapleſs wife.
For me, the vileſt of the ſons of **Thebes**,
Heed thou no farther——once more let me go,
A wand'ring exile from my father's roofs,
From **Thebes**, as erſt from **Corinth**, and explore
That ſacred ſpot on dark Cithæron's brow,
By thoſe who gave me being doom'd my grave
Early as life began; for ah! I feel,
Within this breaſt I feel the dire preſage,
That fate denies me by the common lot
Of man to fall; ſnatch'd from the jaws of death,
To periſh by the ſignal wrath of Jove,
Long treaſur'd for the moment: what that ſtroke
I know not; but deſpair hath arm'd my ſoul——
Deareſt of men, my children I commend
To thy protecting arm; my ſons are firm

In

In health and manhood; they will leaſt require
Thy friendly aid: but oh! my haplefs daughters——
Dear blooming orphans, with ſuch anxious care
Cheriſh'd beneath thefe roofs in royal ſtate;
Fed by my hand, and by my watchful eye
Still guarded: how will thofe poor babes fupport
At once a father's and a mother's lofs?
O take them, prince; O ſhield them with thy power,
And fofter with thy love! Might they be fummon'd?
Might they receive a father's laſt embrace?
To touch them would fufpend my pains: but oh!
To glue my clafping arms around their necks,
Would give me fight, and nerve my limbs anew.
What have I faid of rapture—'tis denied
To this care-broken heart! To weep their fate,
And o'er them hang in fix'd and filent woe,
Is all now left me—but methinks I hear
Sounds fweet and plaintive, like the tender moans
Of thofe dear children: yes, they are my chiidren!
Creon hath gratified my ardent wiſh;
What can I fay—oh torture—

        CRE. To thy command
Obedient, I have brought thy children hither.

                             OED.

OED. Eternal bleffings on thee for this kindnefs!
Come near, my daughters; fhudder not to touch
Your father, and your——brother: view the hands,
Yet red with gore, whofe fury hath confign'd me
To everlafting darknefs, and forbade
The fight of you and heav'n: a king myfelf,
And yet a regicide, by heav'n and man
Alike abhorr'd: approach, and weep my fate,
But do not curfe me with the name of parent.
Yes, to behold your angel fmiles, that once
Gave vigour to my pulfe, is mine no more.
Yet I can weep your fate, and I will weep
In tears of blood warm gufhing from the heart.
With patient fortitude I might have borne
My own difafters, but the fenfe of yours
Hath quite unmann'd me. Whither will ye go
For refpite from your toils, or how affuage
The madnefs of defpair? From public haunts,
And all the gay delights of focial life,
Driv'n with difgrace, your virgin bloom to wafte
In barren folitude, and execrate
The name of father. Ye muft never tafte
The fweets of Hymen, nor with eager eyes
Gaze on a fmiling progeny; for who,

Who

Who will receive pollution to his arms,
Nor fhudder at the black impending guilt
That hangs o'er all the race of Oedipus?
What horror in the tale! An impious fon
Hath flain his father, and, with guilty fires
Flaming, defil'd his mother's facred bed.
Purfu'd with jealous hatred by your fex,
And exil'd by the voice of all mankind——
Thus fhall ye pafs your wretched days, till death,
Thrice welcome, clofe the folitary fcene.
Thou, Creon, thou art left their only friend;
Ah! fuffer not my poor, forfaken babes,
Like vagabonds, to wander o'er the earth
The fport of infamy: dear, generous youth,
Extend thy hands, as pledges of thy faith
And firm fupport: much, O my daughters, much
My heart would utter more, but grief forbids.
This is my only pray'r, that you may live
Refign'd and happy, as your fate will fuffer,
Where heav'n may beft ordain: and may that heav'n
In rich abundance on my childrens head
Shower down the bleffings it denies your fire.

CRE.

CRE. Enough: thy grief transports thee; O! retire
Within the palace.

OED. I obey thee, prince;
Yet shudder to approach that fatal scene
Of all my guilt.

CRE. 'Tis right * thou should'st retire:
Time and events require it.

OED. Know'st thou not
By what dire curses I am bound——

CRE. Declare them.

OED. To leave those roofs, and thou to drive me thence——
O prince, with swiftness execute the task.

CRE. The gods alone can grant thee thy desire.

OED. I am most hateful to those gods.

CRE. Fear not;
They will befriend thee here.

OED. Ah might I hope!

CRE. Thou may'st; I speak with confidence.

OED. Then lead,
Whither thou wilt.

CRE. But let thy children stay.——

OED. Wilt thou bereave me of my children too!

* The original faith, " All things are right on right occasions :" The text seems de-
signedly equivocal and obscure.

CRE.

CRE. Submit—Warn'd by thy fuff'rings, Oh! beware
Of that perverfenefs thou haft rued fo dearly.

CHO. Inhabitants of Thebes, behold your prince,
The mighty Oedipus, whofe foaring thought
Pierc'd the dark riddle of the monfter Sphynx;
Whofe fame * and pow'r, beyond example great,
What fon of Cadmus but with envy view'd ?—
That prince behold, by fad reverfe of fate
Fall'n from his throne of grandeur to the depth
Of abject mifery—Mortal, mark his fate;
Nor him, whom fortune's changeful fmile adorns
With momentary triumphs, call thou bleft,
'Till death decide, and ftamp the name of "happy."

---

* Ὅστις ου ζῆλω.———

As the text now ftands, this is a very difficult paffage, and the tranflations are ambiguous and unfatisfactory. A friend told me of a propofed emendation by the learned Editor of Euripides, Doctor Mufgrave.

Ὅ᾽τ. τις ου ζῆλῳ πολίων῀ης῀υχης επιζλιπιν.

The paffage becomes thus interrogative, and the fenfe is, "whom, who was there of the citizens, but beheld with envy in confequence of his good fortune?" This fenfe I have adopted, as the moft eafy to be tranflated, and beft expreffive of the meaning of Sophocles.

THE END.